The Summer Park Psychics
WANDERING SOUL
WHISPERING HEARTS
LINGERING TOUCH
THE SUMMER PARK PSYCHICS OMNIBUS

Other Works
CRAFTING A WRITER'S LIFE: Building a Foundation

Coming Soon

The Blades of Janus
PERIHELION

Cygnian 7
KRAL
LAR
DORN
BRON
TARN
ROM

Nuar: A Scifi Alien Warriors Romance

Cygnian 7
Book One

Cassandra Chandler

Copyright Page

Nuar: A Scifi Alien Warriors Romance
Cygnian 7, Book One
Copyright © 2021 by Cassandra Chandler
Print ISBN: 978-1-945702-87-7
Digital ISBN: 978-1-945702-86-0

First eBook edition: August 2021
First print edition: August 2021
10 9 8 7 6 5 4 3 2 1

cassandra-chandler.com
P.O. Box 91
Mission, Kansas 66201

Chapter One

Earth was a confusing mess. Nuar couldn't figure out why Kral had dragged all of the warriors in their prism to this backwards planet in the middle of nowhere.

Actually, it was worse than the middle of nowhere. It was well inside Coalition territory. The planet was crawling with Sadirians. The Earthlings themselves were almost identical to the oppressive aliens they had welcomed into their system.

As far as Nuar could tell, none of the Earthlings realized their mistake. They were carrying on their lives as they had since their industrial revolution, almost all of the population not even aware that aliens walked among them, let alone that their planet was one of the few that remained untouched by the galactic war.

Kral should be warning them that they were in a different kind of danger. The Coalition would strip this planet bare of resources and absorb the populace into their own. And that was if Earth was lucky.

With the Tau Centauran Assembly fighting against the Coalition, and winning, by all accounts, the Earthlings could meet with an even darker fate. Nuar felt a twinge of pity for them at the thought of the Tau Ceti colonizing the planet, setting up their wretched spawning pools, and absorbing the populace in their own way—as a food source.

Cygnus-Prime shouldn't be getting anywhere near this mess. So why were Kral and his prism—Nuar included in that honored group—following a Sadirian female on a "tour" of this low-tech, socially stunted planet?

They were heading down a wide walkway that led from the hangar where their ship was located toward a small town called Harbor. The Sadirian's short blonde hair bounced along her shoulders as she walked. She cast a bright smile at them that Nuar absolutely did not trust.

Earth had informally sided with the Coalition of Planets. It remained to be seen whether humans were as corrupt as Sadirians or just too foolish to realize the danger they represented.

Nuar's experience with humans was limited to members of the Department of Homeworld Security. He still hadn't made up his mind about Earthlings, but kept his eyes open as he followed along on the tour.

Perhaps it was a trap instead. That would be interesting.

As much as he believed his people should stay out of Earth's business, he relished the idea of being able to test his strength and skills against a new opponent. The

Earthlings were no threat and their weapons useless against a Cygnian, but they were rumored to have attracted a variety of other species to their planet.

His spirits somewhat lifted, Nuar looked around with renewed interest, seeking challenges or enemies. All he saw was grass, dirt, trees, and a cluster of buildings ahead.

A gentle breeze swept over him, countering the summer temperature—not that it was a problem for Nuar or any of the other Cygnians. Earth's small yellow star cast pitifully low amounts of radiation through the atmosphere. It was no wonder all the life forms on the planet were so weak.

Earth was excessively comfortable.

The sky was unsettling, though. The same blue as Nuar, Dorn, and Rom's skin. The other four members of the prism were a darker blue, with Lar a rich cobalt, like their queen.

"We're so happy that you chose to come," the Sadirian was saying. What was her name again? Right. Vay.

Nuar hoped he wouldn't have to remember it for long. There couldn't be much to see in such a small town. Earth had nothing to offer them.

"We've been getting everything ready for months," Vay continued the steady stream of her conversation. "It's an honor to have your entire prism visiting Earth. Is it true that Cygnians have seven possible eye colors?"

"It is," Lar said.

Nuar felt his chest swell with pride as he thought of the full spectrum represented in his group—a rare complete prism—from Rom's violet eyes to Nuar's own spectral red. The Cygnian population had been dwindling for several generations. Finding fellow warriors whose unique soul-frequencies could harmonize with each others' was becoming more rare.

Finding a soulmate was out of the question.

Vay glanced at the warriors with her, her brow furrowing. Nuar glared when their eyes met, and she quickly looked away.

"Tarn is with the ship," Lar said. "He prefers his engineering bay to new planets."

"I see." Vay's smile was a bit strained. Nuar felt a surge of sympathy for her. He quickly crushed it.

"I was surprised not to see him with the group, since Kral is your crown prince," Vay said.

Bron let out a low growl. The vibration spread out from him, resonating in the plates that covered Nuar's spine. Nuar forced them to stay folded against his back rather than risk tearing through the thin fabric of the Earth clothing Kral had asked them to wear.

"We travel with him because he's our friend, not because he's our prince," Bron said. "He doesn't need bodyguards."

"I didn't mean any offense." Vay's pale blue eyes grew round. "I guess I don't understand the prism bond that well, but I'd love to learn more. I am the cultural liaison, after all. Not that I wouldn't be interested otherwise. I mean, having such a close connection among your group of warriors sounds wonderful."

She barely stopped to breathe as she spoke. Irritating. Primarily because the more she spoke, the harder it was for Nuar to not like her.

He wanted to get this over with. He needed to be... somewhere. Back at his ship, perhaps. Except, he wanted to keep going forward. Deeper into the town.

A strange feeling was nagging at the back of his mind and making him uneasy. It was probably just from knowing there were so many Sadirians and their allies lurking around. Still, it was unsettling.

"I hope you'll accept my apology." Vay clasped her hands in front of her chest as she stopped next to the first building at the edge of town.

Bron had been paying more attention to the environment than the Sadirian leading their group and had to stop abruptly to keep from running into her. Nuar, however, plowed into Bron's back, knocking his fellow warrior forward a few paces.

Bron had to flail his arms and stagger to the side to keep from crushing Vay. It was one of the funniest things Nuar had seen in a while. The group laughed, some of their tense energy unraveling.

"Your turn, then." Bron shoved Nuar, hard.

They both laughed as Nuar nearly lost his footing, flailing in much the same way to avoid the Sadirian in their midst. Dorn stepped in front of her, their security officer always focused on keeping others safe.

It was good to have a distraction. The familiar physical challenge was a much nicer focus than their strange surroundings or that nagging feeling of *need* in the back of Nuar's mind.

"Are you up for an experiment, science officer?" Nuar said with a grin.

Bron arched an eyebrow and asked, "What did you have in mind?"

"Let's see how far I can throw you on this low gravity world," Nuar said.

Bron bared his teeth in a broad smile, setting his feet apart and waiting for Nuar's charge. Rom stepped between them, his hands raised to keep them apart.

"Stop playing around," Rom said.

Nuar straightened. "We're not playing. This is an *experiment*."

"No, this is you being bored and trying to find something to do," Rom said. "As usual."

"I'm the medic for a group of near-invulnerable warriors," Nuar said. "I'm always bored."

Rom stepped right up in Nuar's space, nose-to-nose as he issued his challenge. "Find a more constructive outlet."

The Sadirian chose that moment to join the

conversation. "I think I'm going about this wrong," she said.

She dropped her hands to her sides, glancing back and forth between Rom and Nuar. She pressed her lips together in a determined line, then yelled, "Like I'd think Kral needed a guard!"

She reached out and braced her hands on the closest Cygnian's chest, which happened to be Lar's, and shoved him.

Rather, she tried to. Lar didn't budge.

Nuar had to hand it to the Sadirian, though. She pushed hard enough that she knocked herself backward, landing right against Kral's chest.

Kral caught her to help her keep her balance. He arched an eyebrow at the prism, his orange eyes gleaming with mirth. For a moment, he grinned at them above her head where she couldn't see, then forced his expression to look dour and disapproving again.

"Bron accepts your apology," Kral said, keeping his voice low.

Bron grunted.

Kral bared his teeth, his disapproval most likely becoming real. "Bron accepts your apology." He bit out each word.

With another low growl, Bron inclined his head slightly. "Of course."

"I... Thank you." Vay pulled her lower lip between her

teeth for a moment, then let out a sigh. "I just want you to feel comfortable here."

"Comfort is not an issue." Nuar snorted. "This entire planet is coated in soft things."

He reached over to the building next to them and snapped off a corner of one of the blocks it appeared to be made of. Grinding his fingers against his palm, he watched as the material turned to a russet powder.

"Let's maybe not crush the buildings' bricks," Vay said. "Most of these structures aren't made of advanced durable materials."

"We can see that," Bron said.

"Harbor is an example of what's possible if we all work together," Vay said. "We did our best to preserve the existing Earth structures, improving them with designs proposed by humans and using Vegan technology."

Nuar stifled a snort. He still didn't believe there were actual Vegans on the planet, despite the rumors. He glanced over at Bron, who was also stifling a smirk.

Vay went on, oblivious. "And the Antareans were amazingly helpful in the construction."

The plates running along Nuar's spine started to rise. Judging by how the other warriors' stances changed, most were dealing with the same reaction.

"You used the Antareans?" Lar's tone was thick with disapproval.

"We didn't *use* anyone," Vay said, an intriguing

challenge to her voice. "The Antareans *offered* and the Earthlings of this town gratefully accepted their help in exchange for supplies and resources that have helped the Antarean homeworld immensely."

Vay gestured down the road to a tall building made of similar red blocks—bricks—but wrapped with large brown tunnels built onto the walls in winding spirals. Small plants grew from the tops and sides of the tunnels, and more greenery could be seen on top of the roof.

"You're welcome to talk to them yourself," she said. "Several have decided to settle here and make Harbor their home. They live in that apartment building along with humans, Sadirians, and Vegans."

Nuar saw movement on the roof of the building. Two of the insectoid Antareans walked to the edge of the building, their antennae pointing toward Nuar's group. One was holding a large pot with a plant in it. They both lifted some of their many arms and waved.

"Greetings, Vay," one of them shouted.

"Hello Sisters," Vay yelled, waving back. "Your rooftop garden is looking great!"

"Thank you," the other Antarean replied. Their giant, segmented eyes strobed a happy pink. "We look forward to planting Lian's latest seedlings once they are ready." They waved again before heading back toward the center of the roof and out of sight.

Vay turned to the prism and said, "Please don't mistake

the Coalition for the High Council. The High Council is gone and…" she lifted her chin, "good riddance to them."

With every word, Nuar liked her more, no matter how much he didn't want to. His desire to leave the planet also grew. They should not be getting involved in any of this.

"The *Coalition* does not take advantage of sentients," Vay said. "We take care of each other. We work—and live —together. That's Harbor. And if you don't like it…" She seemed to struggle to find the right word. When she did, she stiffened her spine and crossed her arms over her chest. "Tough cookies."

Lar looked at Kral and mouthed, "Tough cookies?"

Kral laughed. Nuar felt his spine plates relax. He still didn't trust the Coalition, but this Sadirian… This Sadirian, he liked.

The High Council might be gone, but their influence most likely remained among their people. They couldn't have changed that much in such a short amount of time.

"The town is a fine accomplishment," Kral said. "It's good to see these sentients working together."

"We're very proud of what we've done here," Vay said.

"As you should be." Kral laughed again, then pulled Vay against his side with an arm draped over her shoulders. Her eyes widened, but she didn't protest.

"One thing, though," Kral said. "What are cookies?"

Vay beamed at him, her eyes crinkling at the corners.

"Cygnus X, they are the best thing in the universe." She clamped a hand over her mouth for a moment, then said, "Pardon my language."

Kral just smiled.

"Are they a weapon?" Bron asked.

She pinched her lips between her teeth, then burst out with a laugh. "No, they're a food. A delicious food. We can pick some up at the bakery. It's just down the street."

They started along the paved path again, passing buildings with clear viewports that made up most of their front walls. Nuar glanced around as Vay described the operations within them, not really listening.

His gaze lit on a large, white, multi-armed form across the street. Was that a Lyrian?

"I'll catch up in a moment," Nuar said.

Bron shrugged, then followed Vay and the other warriors into one of the buildings.

Excitement teased the edges of Nuar's nerves. His hearts pounded a dual beat in either side of his chest.

Finally, something of interest.

Lyrians rarely left their planet. Nuar had never seen one, though he'd studied everything he could about them.

Lyrians could camouflage themselves so well, they would be undetectable through any physical or technological means. Not even Cygnian holographic technology could rival a Lyrian's natural defense.

Their strength and resilience was legendary. This one

was seven feet tall—as tall as Nuar—but three times as thick in the chest.

Few Cygnians had ever had a chance to try their might against a Lyrian.

Nuar crossed the street quickly, coming up behind the Lyrian as he turned around a corner. Nuar hurried to catch up with him.

The moment Nuar rounded the corner, four strong hands gripped him and lifted him off his feet. He found himself staring into eyes as dark blue as Tarn's, set in a pale blue face surrounded by bristling white fur.

The Lyrian pulled his lips back from his many small, serrated teeth in a smile. "Hello, Cygnian," he said. "Would you care to explain why you're trying to sneak up on me?

Nuar laughed. "Cygnians don't sneak. I was approaching you to introduce myself. I am Nuar."

The Lyrian pursed his lips and snorted out a breath through the nostrils in his flat face. His winglike ears twitched as he set Nuar down and released him.

"I'm Craig," the Lyrian said.

"Well met, Craig." Nuar extended his hand.

Craig's brow ridge arched on one side. He gripped Nuar's hand in the Earth-style greeting Nuar had been trained to use, but then clasped Nuar's elbow with one of his other hands.

"Are you supposed to be here, Nuar?" Craig asked.

"Vay's been talking for weeks about the tour she has planned for you all."

Nuar waved his free hand dismissively. "My prism can sense where I am. And I doubt the Sadirian will even notice my departure."

"Hmm." Craig tightened his grips. "Interesting that you call her 'the Sadirian,' when you know she has a name."

"I also know she's with the Coalition." Nuar tightened his grip as well. Tighter than the grip he'd used to pulverize the brick. The Lyrian was unfazed.

Craig smirked. "Did you also know that Vay is my daughter?"

Nuar felt his jaw drop. The Coalition was infamous for their genetic experiments, but creating a Sadirian linked with Lyrian DNA? How had the Coalition even obtained it?

Nuar had thought that the Lyrians were one of the few sentient species fortunate enough to have eluded the High Council's lust for more genetic material to experiment upon. Then again, until recently, Nuar had thought the Cygnians had managed to escape that fate as well. He was wrong.

His spines began to rise again at the thought of what the High Council had done to one of their own. Craig's grip tightened further, perhaps noticing Nuar's distress.

Nuar stammered a few half-formed words, his mind refusing to provide anything helpful besides, "How?"

"This planet has a very strange effect on unmated sentients," Craig said. His voice became a bit wistful as he went on. "My mate and I adopted an orphaned human we found wandering the woods alone and unprotected. When he met Vay, they pair-bonded. They are now married, both according to Sadirian and Earth customs."

"I see," Nuar said. That made a lot more sense than the scenarios he'd been considering.

Craig pulled Nuar closer, so that their faces were inches apart. "I'm not sure you do. Vay has been very excited about today. She's worked tirelessly to prepare for your arrival, barely having time to spend with our family and our new nestling. And yet, you're here, and she's there. Which I'm concerned might disappoint her."

Nuar smiled, his hearts pounding at the thought of a true challenge. "If you'd like, you're welcome to try to get me from here to there."

Craig's lips pulled into a toothy smile again. "I would love to."

Chapter Two

Craig had better get back soon.

Lian sighed as she slouched down further on the bench where she waited. Her ponytail holder had fallen out at some point, letting her hair drape over the back of the bench.

She closed her eyes for a moment and took a deep breath. The scent of fresh earth mingled with the flowers blooming in the greenhouse—a greenhouse she had designed, in conjunction with her best friend Olivia's plans for the attached library.

The foliage had been set up so that it seemed like you were walking on a meandering path, when the area really wasn't that big. There were several little alcoves where you could sit and read a book while listening to birds or trickling water from fountains made to look like real springs.

In the library part of the building, shelves made of a fabricated material that looked and felt exactly like dark mahogany stood in curved rows that were somehow both orderly and natural. The floor that wove between them in stream-like patterns was covered in something that looked like bamboo tiles, but was supposedly nearly indestructible.

Living in the only town on Earth that had been secretly colonized by aliens definitely had big advantages. When Lian thought about everyone going about their lives, business as usual, with no knowledge that Earth wasn't alone in the universe...

Well, she was really grateful she lived in Harbor, Kansas.

The tiles in the library could be lifted out and reused indefinitely. They were also easy to clean, as Lian had recently discovered.

Craig and Barbara had gone to the ice cream parlor on Main Street before dropping Ellie off for Lian to babysit. It was amazing how much vanilla praline with peanut butter ripple the baby Lyrian had managed to get into her fluffy white fur without anybody noticing.

Scratch that. Lian's St. Bernard, Ed, had noticed. He'd been thrilled to try to lick Ellie clean while she scampered around messing up the floor. Lian was pretty sure Ed thought Ellie was some kind of strange puppy.

Now, Ellie was splayed on Lian's chest as Lian leaned back on the bench that she and her father had finished a few weeks ago. It was the first piece of furniture he'd been able to build in over a decade.

That was the biggest bonus to allowing aliens to join

them in Harbor. The aliens among them had also built an incredible hospital and were sharing their medical technology with the town.

Lian's father had had crippling arthritis in his hands. He didn't complain about it, but she knew he missed his woodworking. Now, he spent every day in his garage, making beautiful pieces that he shipped all over the world.

Lian ran her fingertips over a small lizard he'd engraved on the arm of the bench. Every piece had a similar design. It was his way of thanking the Vegans—the small, reptilian aliens responsible for the technology that had helped him.

Lian's grandmother was out of the nursing home and back at work in the garden. They even worked in the greenhouse together some days. It was a dream come true. Lian couldn't wait for the rest of the planet to be ready to welcome the aliens who had become her friends, though she knew it would probably be a while.

Planets at Earth's level of social development who suddenly had everything they could ever need dropped into their lap usually ended up tearing themselves apart. The people in power wouldn't want to give up their hold on others and often resorted to catastrophic measures to do so.

Lian could understand why the aliens living with them were hesitant to share their tech beyond Harbor's city limits.

But someday…

In the meantime, Lian would enjoy her front row seat to the sci-fi extravaganza that her life had become. She was one of the few humans that Craig and Barbara trusted to watch their adorable baby Lyrian—otherwise known as Space-Sasquatches.

The nestling had a broad mouth, two flat nostrils in the center of her face, and big blue eyes that Lian had trouble saying 'no' to. Her fur was white and her skin pale blue.

Ellie had the most adorable ears that looked like little bat wings. They twitched in her sleep sometimes. She also still had her "baby tentacles" and she'd only just grown her first set of arms.

Living with aliens was kind of weird.

A breeze flowed over Lian's skin, making it break out in goosebumps. Her stomach suddenly felt as though it was full of butterflies and her breath caught in her chest.

More of the goosebumps trickled down her spine and spread over her back. What the heck was going on?

She looked around, but didn't see anyone.

Thanks to the super-advanced technology used to build the greenhouse, the walls weren't really walls, they were energy fields. Lian had no idea how that worked, but the walls could be deactivated—like they were now—letting in breezes and fresh air and…something else.

She hugged Ellie closer to her chest and sat up straighter. Energy crackled over her skin, electric and not unpleasant. Not unpleasant at all, actually.

Warmth spread through her belly. Her heart sped.

"What the hell?" she murmured.

"Did you say something?"

Lian started at the unexpected voice behind her. She leapt up, turning as she did. Gary was standing behind her, holding a stack of books.

His eyes widened when he saw the Lyrian still sleeping and clinging to Lian's chest. Lian hugged Ellie a little closer.

Gary always tended to show up when Lian was babysitting Ellie. It was creepy. Lian wished she had brought Ed out to the greenhouse with her, but the muggy air was too hot for the shaggy dog to stand for long.

"I'm so sorry," Gary whispered. "I came to return these."

"It's okay," Lian said, keeping her voice as low as possible. She was already keyed up to the Nth degree. Gary's presence only made it worse.

Gary smiled and nodded, his eyes never leaving Ellie. "Babysitting again?"

He was being creepier than usual. Or maybe it seemed worse because of whatever had Lian on edge. She felt like she was waiting for something she didn't understand.

A loud crash sounded on the street, followed by a car alarm. Lian yelped.

"What was that?" Gary moved closer, which oddly

made Lian even less at ease.

"I have no idea."

Ellie blinked up at Lian with bleary eyes. One of the blue-and-white striped tentacles attached to her sides whipped up to rub them.

"It's okay," Lian said. "It's gonna be okay."

Lian wasn't sure how convincing she sounded. She had no idea what was going on.

"You don't think it's the Cygnians, do you?" Gary asked.

Lian's blood turned cold.

The other purpose of Harbor was to provide a neutral meeting place for aliens who might be having a little trouble getting along. The theory was that it would teach those aliens about Earth and show them an example of many cultures existing side-by-side.

The Cygnians were scheduled to arrive today.

They were incredibly strong, almost indestructible, and all of them were warriors. They rarely left their homeworld and were one of the few factions that was remaining neutral in some huge space war that was going on.

Earth hadn't been touched by the war yet, thanks to the Vegan's protection. Lian still worried about whether that protection would really be able to keep her planet safe. She also worried about keeping most of the planet in the dark about aliens when there was so much potential for everyone to find out in a truly unpleasant way.

She heard another crash—this one much closer. A lamppost smashed into the sidewalk.

Ed was in the library. Lian could hear him barking through the side entrance that connected the library to the greenhouse.

"We should get Ellie inside where it's safe," Gary said.

Lian wasn't entirely sure anyplace was safe, but she nodded anyway and followed him.

Just as they reached the door, there was a horrible, screeching roar. Something huge and white hurtled through the greenhouse. It hit the ground, tearing up plants and pathways and leaving a deep furrow in the ground behind it.

"Craig…" Lian said.

Shaking bits of debris from his fur, Craig pushed himself up on his four arms, then rose and turned toward the street. His lips were pulled back in a smile she'd never seen from him, revealing rows of tiny, sharp teeth.

He plucked a length of ivy from his chest and said, "Oh, it's on now."

Instead of running to the street, he turned and dropped to all…sixes. His many arms pounded into the soft ground, creating more divots as he charged across the garden area to the far side of the greenhouse. There was a small, wrought iron table and chair set on that side.

Lian opened the door to the library. Ed bounded out,

his deep woof both reassuring and making her worry more. She didn't want him getting into this.

She shoved Ed back into the library, following him into the cooler building. Peeling the Lyrian baby's many limbs from her torso, she set Ellie on Ed's back. Ellie immediately let out a squeal of delight.

Ed barked a few times and opened his mouth in a huge, slobbery smile. He started spinning in circles, trying to lick the baby Lyrian. It was their favorite game and should keep them out of trouble for at least a few minutes.

Hopefully.

"Fight or hide," Lian shouted to Gary, who had also followed her into the building. "Your choice."

She ran back into the greenhouse, pulling the door shut behind her. She headed straight toward her tool area.

Ed would keep Ellie safe, and Lian couldn't leave Craig to face whatever this was alone. She grabbed a heavy, metal-headed rake.

Glancing around, she saw that Gary was nowhere to be seen. He must have decided to stay inside.

It was just her then. Fine.

Adrenaline coursed through her, heightening the goosebumps that were still all over her. Her back especially felt electrified all down her spine. She didn't have time to think about it.

She gripped her rake and turned toward the fight, assessing the new damage and looking for Craig's opponent. It wasn't hard to spot him.

Tall, muscled, and very, very blue, the Cygnian warrior stood at the far end of what had been the carefully landscaped garden. His eyes were a vibrant red.

Her mouth went dry and more of those strange goosebumps swept over her skin. The feeling of butterflies in her stomach intensified and she found herself taking a step toward him before she stopped herself.

The Cygnian's dark blue hair was short and his chiseled jaw covered in sapphire stubble. He had the broadest shoulders she'd ever seen, and his seven-foot something frame was packed with muscle.

He was utterly gorgeous.

His gaze turned to her, and she swore his eyes started to glow.

"Hey, Nuar," Craig said. "Catch."

Two of the wrought iron chairs flew across the greenhouse, straight toward the Cygnian. He knocked the first one aside, but the other hit him in the chest—and bounced off.

Just bounced right off. The guy didn't even flinch.

"Damn," Lian whispered.

The Cygnian locked his gaze on her again, then started forward.

Chapter Three

What was this captivating life form? Nuar should have been repulsed given how much she resembled a Sadirian. But then, all Earthlings did. The two alien species were genetically nearly identical. Thankfully, their cultures were vastly different.

Earthlings also tended to have more variance in their bodies, since they were created naturally and not genetically engineered. This female's body looked soft. Her curves were distracting, as was the rest of her.

Her hair was lustrous black, thick and straight. Her eyes were a warm chestnut brown and seemed to spark with intelligence and...was it fury? That emotion would match the deep frown on her lips and the way her jaw was clenched tight.

She held a stick that was almost as tall as she was. A row of metal prongs topped her weapon.

Nuar struck his wristbands together as he approached her, the vibration of the metal reverberating through his body. He hummed a low note to activate their scanning function, then spread his arms, allowing them better access to gather data.

The female—he was certain of that at least—lurched back. She lifted the primitive weapon she held and brandished it toward him.

"If you're looking for a hug, you're barking up the wrong tree," she said.

Her voice was low and had a rasp that set his spine plates tingling. He tried to process what she was saying, the language imprinted in his mind having trouble with the idiomatic expression.

Barking was the sound dogs made. He knew that because of his interactions with his Earth-friend Buddy's dog. Why would a dog bark up any tree? Unless perhaps they had cornered an opponent in one.

He understood why she might think he sought a hug, with his arms outstretched as they were. What he didn't understand was why he actually liked the idea of holding her.

He stopped when they were close. Instead of lifting her weapon to strike him, she lowered it a bit.

Her chest rose and fell with quick breaths and her full lips parted as she stared at him. His spine plates started to rise and his groin tightened.

A hologram of her readings appeared above his right wristband. It took effort to look away from her to interpret them.

Her circulatory system was racing. Neural activity was

higher than expected for either species she might be. Blood flow was increasing to her face, neck, breasts, and between her legs.

Interesting, especially given his response to her.

The female glanced over at the hologram, her lips snapping back to a frown. She struck his wristband with her weapon, scattering the image.

"Hey, that's private," she said.

"I'm a medic."

She lifted the weapon higher. "You're not *my* medic, so back off."

"Do you believe that puny little stick will work against me?"

"It won't have to," she said, smirking.

Four strong hands clamped on Nuar's arms and spun him around.

"Remember me?" Craig stepped in close and head butted Nuar.

Nuar staggered, but managed to grab two of Craig's arms. He threw himself backward, taking Craig with him. Nuar planted his feet in Craig's stomach and flipped his huge opponent over his head.

Unfortunately, Craig had two more arms. The Lyrian dug his fingers into the soil, gouging deep furrows as he stopped his momentum. Then he launched himself back at Nuar.

Craig's shoulder struck Nuar's chest. The impact

knocked Nuar through a grouping of plants. Their leaves shredded as he flailed his arms to keep his balance.

He shifted his weight and was just about to launch himself forward when something flicked the back of his head. He turned to see the female standing behind him. Her eyebrows were high on her forehead as she stared at her weapon. It had broken off on one end. She glanced at the ground, where the top half lay.

Had she just broken that over his head?

Nuar laughed. "What a fierce little female you are. But this doesn't concern you."

"Don't call me little," she said, her voice low and strong. "My name is Lian."

An odd frisson of pleasure swept down his spine.

"And this absolutely concerns me," Lian continued. "You're destroying my greenhouse."

"What's a green—"

Before he could finish his question, Craig crashed into Nuar's side and sent him flying. Nuar hit one of the pillars of metal generating the interlacing energy fields above them. The energy field let out a brief fizz of static, but the pillar held. Nuar bounced off of it and landed on his back in a pile of soft, flowering greenery.

"I win," Craig yelled. "That's five times I sent you to the ground."

Nuar flipped to his feet. "That was four. We've only tied."

Craig started counting with his fingers. "I knocked you to the ground on the sidewalk, the car, the table in front of the coffee shop across the street—"

"The car doesn't count," Nuar said. "Slamming me down on a vehicle is not the same as taking me to the ground."

"It *is* the same," Craig yelled.

"Listen, you—" Nuar cut off his sentence as something bounced off the back of his head. He glanced down to see the other half of Lian's weapon at his feet. Apparently, she'd thrown it at him.

"A game?" she cried. "This was a *game*?"

Some of the color leached from Craig's face. "I can explain," he said.

While Craig was distracted, Nuar made his move. He sprang forward, grabbing the Lyrian under his lower set of arms and lifting Craig above his head.

"Now, we will have a true victor," Nuar shouted. He turned away from Lian to keep her safe and threw Craig across the space.

"Not the bench!" she shrieked.

The anguish in her voice tore at Nuar's soul. Nuar might have been able to use his wristbands to alter Craig's path, but there was no time.

Craig's momentum carried him straight toward a bench nestled among some plants. The bench shattered from the impact, breaking into splinters that flew through the air.

The Lyrian's arms hit the plants surrounding it, crushing them.

No one moved. Craig remained lying in the debris, his eyes wide as he stared at Lian. The only sound was her harsh breathing and the creaking of one of the pots hanging behind her as it swung lop-sided from a single surviving chain attached to the support structure above.

"Um..." Craig said. "I'm here to pick up Ellie."

Nuar watched intently as Lian turned and walked to a door that led to a connected building. She pulled it open and stood to one side.

A large creature walked out with a baby Lyrian riding it. The mount was covered in shaggy fur, had long ears on the sides of its head, and its lips hung down past its chin. Its back was reddish and its legs and belly white. Another line of white fur ran between its eyes and all around its mouth, contrasting with its dark nose.

It let out a deep, "Woof!" as it walked toward Craig.

The Lyrian infant on its back held on to tufts of the creature's fur with her hands and feet. The tentacles where her lower arms would eventually grow waved in the air as she laughed. She looked happier than Nuar thought he'd ever seen a life form.

It only made the misery and rage on Lian's face more noticeable.

"Ellie." Craig picked up his daughter and cradled her against his chest. "There's my little nestling."

Ellie smiled at first, but then started fidgeting, trying to get back to her mount. One of her tentacles kept smacking Craig in the face as she reached toward the beast.

"Ed," Lian said. "Go inside."

The creature glanced up at Nuar and sniffed the air, then turned and headed back into the building.

Another awkward silence descended, though this time, the main sound was the unhappy grunts of the Lyrian nestling.

"About the greenhouse," Craig said.

"What about the greenhouse, Craig?" Lian crossed her arms over her chest and glared at him.

The last chain supporting the hanging container behind her snapped. The pot hit the ground and shattered, dirt exploding out from it and parts of the plant within making an ominous crunch.

Lian closed her eyes and took a deep breath. When she opened her eyes again, they glimmered strangely. The sight caused a dull ache to radiate from Nuar's hearts through his torso.

"You need to take Ellie home." Lian's voice was even lower than it had been before. "When she is safely with Barbara, you will come back here so I can kick your ass properly."

"Lian—" Craig said.

Lian held up a finger and cocked her head to the side, not looking at him. "I'm going to count to five. Then I start using words you do not want your baby girl to hear. You get me?"

"I do," Craig said. "And I'm sorry. We were carried away and—"

"One. Two." Lian's voice rose with each number as she counted, ticking them off with a finger. "Three."

Speaking so quickly that his words blurred together, Craig said, "And I'll be back as soon as possible to help clean up this mess." He bolted out onto the sidewalk and disappeared from view.

Had the Lyrian actually been afraid of this small sentient? Nuar could hardly believe it. And yet, she seemed to be having a strange influence on Nuar himself.

Lian bowed her head, her hair forming a screen that hid most of her face from view. She let her arm drop back to her side. Both of her hands were curled into fists.

Nuar had no idea what to do. He glanced around at the disturbed earth and the green leaves and colorful petals strewn about.

"I suppose I should be going as well," Nuar said.

Lian's head snapped up, her gaze boring into him. "Oh, you should? Really? You do all of this—" she gestured broadly, taking in the devastation around her— "and then decide it's time to just take off. Maybe have a lovely afternoon stroll. Is that it?"

"I have no idea how to address this," Nuar said.

"So, you're just going to run away?"

He snarled, his spine plates rising and vibrating. He felt the thin fabric of his Earth clothing stretch. A wave of warning sound rippled out from him, resonating with the metal supports and letting out a high chime.

Lian didn't back down. Her eyes widened, and her lips parted—why could he not seem to look away from them? But then she snapped her mouth shut and redoubled her glare. The challenge she presented was irresistible.

Nuar stalked toward her, stopping when they stood close. "I am from a planet where everything is made of stone and crystal. How was I supposed to know how delicate everything on Earth is?"

"Delicate?" she gasped. "How's this for delicate, you jackass!"

Lian pulled her fist back, then smashed it into his cheek. Her eyes widened and her mouth dropped open. The anger in her expression turned to pain.

"Ffff..farfegnugen!" she shouted.

Nuar was pretty sure his translation session was off on that one. He didn't need to understand her words to know she was still enraged.

"My presence here is only upsetting you more," he said. "I should go."

But as he thought about it, he didn't want to leave. Which was strange, because he should.

"I can ask the other Cygnian warriors for assistance," he said. "I don't know where to begin—"

"You start by saying you're sorry," she yelled.

She shook her hand. Her eyebrows rose and her mouth dropped open.

"Ow ow ow ow…" She brought her hand close to her chest, curling around it protectively.

"You're injured."

"Duh," she yelled. "You didn't tell me that you *also* are made of stone and crystal, you jerk."

"I'm not. But the intense gravity and radiation of our home system has made our skin and tissues evolve to be extremely dense."

"I have news for you—that's not all that's dense about you."

A growl built in his chest, but he was able to keep it low enough she wouldn't hear. At least, she shouldn't have been able to hear it. She stiffened and eyed him even more warily.

"Let me see your hand," he said.

"No."

If saying he was sorry was the beginning of reparations for this, then perhaps Earthlings put a high value on words. He thought back over his cultural training sessions, looking for a word that could help.

"Please," he said.

She scowled at him.

Perhaps a little more convincing was needed. He felt his spine plates lower as he forced his voice to be calm.

"I'm a medic, remember?" he said. "Now let me see."

"Fine, but only because it really hurts." She was still glaring, but she slowly extended her hand.

Nuar lifted his arms and struck his wristbands together. The metal let out a sharp clang. The vibration continued as he activated their scanning function. He held his arms on either side of her hand, rotating them so that he could get a complete view of her physiology.

"What the hell are you doing?" she asked.

If he wasn't mistaken, there was a hint of curiosity in her voice. At the very least, she didn't sound as angry.

"I'm scanning you." He hummed a new note, and a three-dimensional holographic display of her arm appeared a few inches above it. He let out a surprised gasp. "Your hand is broken in three places."

The lines of the fractures were illuminated in bright white light.

"What a surprise." Lian started to pull back.

"Hold still."

She glared at him.

"Please," he said, trying to make his voice gentler. "For just a few moments."

Her eyebrows lowered, but she slowly moved her hand back to where it had been.

"How hard did you hit me?" he asked, more to distract her while he worked than anything else.

"As hard as I could," she said.

He chuckled. It was rare that he was able to treat such an injury. He knew the basics of fixing broken bones, but for a Cygnian to suffer an injury like this... He couldn't think of a scenario that would cause it.

His bracers cast light on her hand, the wavelength providing healing radiation that penetrated to her bones. At the same time, they sent a vibration to activate and accelerate her body's own healing potential.

"What is that?" she said, and this time, he was certain her voice was laced with curiosity.

"It's a healing field. Cygnian technology is founded on light and vibration. Much of it is in spectra and bandwidths you can't perceive, but they have an impact on your physiology."

"That's amazing." She carefully extended her fingers. "It doesn't hurt at all anymore."

Her scowl softened into a smile as she stared at her hand, testing out more movement. The sight of that slight smile made his hearts beat more strongly. Something in his chest coiled tight, as if readying itself for action. But what?

The healing complete, he deactivated his wristbands and let his arms drop to his sides.

"See?" he said. "I'm not such a bad guy after all."

The ghost of her smile vanished instantly. Her gaze snapped back to his as she scowled.

"I would go with, 'Not so inept at fixing the messes he

causes,'" she said.

He stepped closer, intent on… He wasn't quite sure. Before he could say anything, someone cleared their throat nearby.

"Sorry," the male said. "I was just checking to make sure everyone is okay. Ed came back in without Ellie."

"Ellie went home with Craig." There was an edge to Lian's voice, as if she didn't like the male very much.

"What happened out here?" he asked, looking around. "Do you need help?"

Nuar's spine plates rose. This male didn't need to help Lian. Nuar would do it.

As soon as he figured out how.

"This is none of your concern and your assistance is not required," Nuar said.

Lian turned back to him and started jabbing Nuar in the chest as she spoke. "*Gary* lives in Harbor and this is *his* library and *his* community greenhouse so it is *absolutely* his concern."

She poked Nuar one last time when she was done speaking, her brow furrowed.

"Well, *I* am the one who made this mess and so *I* will figure out how to fix it," Nuar said, poking her chest just as she'd done to him.

Her eyes widened and her mouth dropped open on a gasp. Then, amazingly, her glare intensified further as she pulled her hand back to hit him. Again.

This time, he saw it coming and was able to catch her wrist before impact. His spine plates vibrated and he pulled her closer, so that her body was almost touching his. Waves of sensation coated his skin, resonating deep within him.

That glare of hers. It could melt the iciest comet. He wanted to reach up and touch her, to run his fingers along her cheek. He wanted to lay her down upon the soft ground and…claim her.

Claim her as his.

Holding onto her, the warmth of her skin, the beating of her pulse beneath his hand, intensified the feeling. Pressure shifted in his chest. His hearts seemed to be fighting against each other with their alternating beats, each pounding faster and faster until they joined with hers —in unison.

For the first time in his life, his hearts beat as one.

Chapter Four

Gazing meaningfully into each others' eyes was stupid. At least, Lian had always thought so. At the moment, she was starting to reconsider.

Anyway, this was *glaring*, not gazing. She absolutely hated this guy.

Still, the skin on her back was prickling with the best goosebumps of her life. They stretched down her arms and legs and even spread to that very special spot that hadn't seen any action in a depressingly long amount of time.

Lust battling with her anger wasn't surprising. He was tall, ripped, and she could totally get into that blue. What was weird was that he seemed to be having a similar reaction to her. It was like they didn't know whether they wanted to fight or screw.

Fight. Definitely fight.

She hated him. He had destroyed her greenhouse.

It didn't matter that he had a gorgeous jawline and was ripped and towered over her in a way that didn't make her feel intimidated but was somehow unbelievably sexy. He didn't seem put off by her temper or her mouth, either.

That last part was a little harder for her to dismiss. Most men would have run screaming to the hills by now.

"Excuse me," Gary said, with the worst timing ever. "You might not know, but it's considered socially unacceptable to touch a woman there. I mean, unless you're...involved. And even then, you wouldn't do it in public. Or with quite that technique."

Lian slowly turned her glare on Gary.

"Are you finished?" she asked.

"I'll...just be going," Gary said.

He lifted his hand to wave, and Lian noticed blood running down his palm.

"Gary, what the hell?" She tried to walk away from Nuar, but he kept his grip on her wrist.

Fury rose up in her. She pushed as much murderous intent as she could into her gaze and said, "If you do not let go of me immediately, I swear to god, I will find a way to end you."

Nuar's eyes narrowed and his lips twitched at the corners.

Did he think her threatening him was funny? Everyone had been calling them Cygnian *warriors*, so maybe he considered that flirting.

Dammit, she shouldn't care what he thought.

Nuar let go of her, leaving her spinning in her own thoughts. She pulled her attention to Gary and his mysterious injury.

"What happened?" she asked, heading over to him.

"Oh, it's nothing," he said. "I thought Ellie would like to be held by someone with arms since her parents have so many of them. Ed did not approve."

"Ed did this?" Her stomach felt like it was flooded with ice. "I'm so sorry. He's never done anything like that before."

"It's okay," Gary said. "Ed is a good dog. He was just watching out for Ellie. I should have known better."

"Still…"

Gary reached out with his non-bitten hand and cupped Lian's elbow. "Really, it's okay."

"Well, this big blue guy says he's a doctor and he healed me, so—" Lian turned to Nuar and her voice stuck in her throat.

The "big blue guy" had his head lowered so that he was looking at them from below his furrowed brow with eyes that were glowing very, very red. The air around him pulsed with a menacing vibration.

His upper lip curled in a snarl that revealed blazingly white and surprisingly sharp teeth. Were they kind of serrated?

A shiver passed through her as she imagined what it would feel like to have those teeth gently raked over her skin.

What the actual fuck, Lian? Get it together!

"It's fine," Gary said, backing away. "I'm just going to

go wash it off. I'll let it heal the old fashioned way." As soon as his back hit the door, he fumbled for the handle to open it, then fled into the library.

Lian turned around and slapped Nuar's chest. "What the hell is wrong with you?" she shouted. "You could have helped him."

"He didn't want my help."

"Because you scared the crap out of him."

"He should *not* have touched you," Nuar said, a strange clip to the words.

"You don't *get* to say that," she said, mocking his cadence. "I don't give a shit if you Cygnians are some kind of super scary alien badass warrior guys. You are not allowed to go around destroying buildings and intimidating people."

He stared at her for a few moments, then said, "Badass?"

"Ugh. You're impossible."

She started to move away, and he grabbed her fucking wrist again.

It wouldn't have been quite as bad if her body would stop sending her those freaking confusing signals. Another thrill shot through her at his touch, heat pooling low in her belly.

Not. Okay.

She took a deep breath and let it out slowly to calm herself.

"Nuar," she said, forcing her voice to stay level. "I understand that you are from another planet and you do things differently there. We had a whole class on it."

He actually smirked. She wanted to slap it off his face, but knew that would be both futile and counterproductive. She needed to model the behavior she wanted, after all. Which, unfortunately, meant getting her own runaway temper in check—something she was not very good at.

"On Earth, in Harbor, we do not touch women's breasts or…other areas," she gestured vaguely, hoping he'd get the point, "without their express consent. That means you have to ask first and they have to very clearly say, 'Yes, you may touch me there.' And we do not grab people and force them to stay where we want them to be. Ask before you touch. We use our words."

She tried not to sound too condescending with that last part and failed pretty miserably.

Nuar stepped closer to her. Her breath caught in her chest.

Normally, if a guy did something like that, she'd be freaked out and scared. With Nuar, she somehow knew he wouldn't hurt her. That didn't mean he wasn't royally pissing her off.

To make things more confusing and irritating, part of her actually liked his proximity. A mindless, lust-driven, stupid part of her that she would have words with as soon as she could get some distance from this mess.

He let go of her wrist suddenly.

Stepping back, he bowed, and said, "For all of the lapses in my behavior, as well as the damage caused here, I am deeply sorry."

"Wow, I was not expecting that."

He didn't seem like the apologizing type.

She glanced around at the mess, trying to decide what to do next. The silence started to get awkward. When she looked up at Nuar, he was smiling. The sight ticked her off.

Crossing her arms, she said, "So, what's your plan for making it right?"

"First, I will ask for permission to touch you."

Her eyes widened and heat rocketed right to her core. Again, that had not been what she'd expected.

"I was talking about the greenhouse," she said, gesturing to the space.

"I have no idea," he said. "But do I have permission to touch you while I figure it out?"

"What?" She wanted to take a step back, but her feet felt like they were rooted to the spot. "No."

Well, that wiped the smile off his face. The victory felt hollow. Her skin tingled just from the thought of his touch.

"Look, we need to fix this," she said.

"That's what I'm trying to do."

"Great. Then grab a broom."

"What's a broom?"

She scrunched her lips together to keep from yelling at him. Of course he didn't know what a broom was.

She stalked over to the tool area and picked up a broom, then headed back to him. Before handing it over, she figured she should show him how to use the thing.

"You sweep the bristles like this to gather dirt and debris in one place," she said.

"Then what do I do with it?"

"We'll get a dustpan and probably put it in the compost." She looked around at the broken plants, the damage hitting her anew.

So much loss. So much that they'd worked for just... gone.

Even with the Vegans' technology, it had taken months for the plants to reach this level of fullness and growth. All that progress had been wiped out.

She looked over to where the bench had been and her eyes blurred as they filled with tears. That was the worst part of it all. The plants could regrow, but the bench...

"My dad and I built that bench together," she said, her voice raspy. "The Vegans had just finished their last healing session with him. Before that, his arthritis was too bad for him to hold tools. He was so happy to be able to contribute something to the community. And now it's gone."

Why did she say that? She wasn't the over-sharing type.

"I am truly sorry," Nuar said, his voice tight. "Please. May I touch you?"

She gripped the broom with a white-knuckled grip. Dammit, it was so tempting. Too tempting.

She let the broom drop and turned to him, wrapping her arms around his waist.

Nuar was cooler than she'd expected. But definitely... firm. Very firm.

He'd said he wasn't made of stone. As unyielding as his skin was, it felt like he was. She could also feel some sort of ridges along his spine through the thin fabric of his shirt and had to keep herself from running her fingers over them.

It was weird that he was wearing jeans and a T-shirt. The Cygnians must be trying to fit in. She wondered what was behind that.

She also wondered why he wasn't holding her like she was holding him. The moment she'd wrapped her arms around him, he'd quickly lifted his hands out to the sides.

"Lian," he said, his voice pleading. "May I please touch you?"

Oh wow. He was still waiting for permission. He had definitely taken her admonishment seriously.

"Yes, you may." She quickly added, "Just this once."

His arms wrapped around her, pulling her closer against his body.

How had this started? She couldn't remember.

All she knew was the strength of his arms and how gently they held her, the feel of his palms on her back, the rock-wall of his chest. She had never felt so safe in her life.

And then the tingling kicked in.

More of those delicious goosebumps spread over her arms, her back, her stomach and chest and…other places. They went deeper than her skin.

Her body was alive in a way it had never been before. She felt it all the way to her bones.

She held him tighter, energy coiling deep in her belly, pooling between her legs. Her hands moved over his back, tracing the outline of his spine.

There were definitely ridges there. They quivered beneath her touch.

Nuar groaned, his hands clutching her shirt in fists. Other parts of him became even firmer.

Holy crap.

Yeah, that was…impressive. But only a distraction from everything else she was experiencing.

Her chest felt over-full, like her heart was expanding to fill more space than usual. Like it was trying to reach out to him.

Ugh, when had she become so corny?

And yet…

"Lian," Nuar said, his voice definitely raspy.

She looked up at him, blinking against the bright red

light shining from his eyes.

"May I kiss you?" he asked.

No. Absolutely not. She hated him.

"Sure," she said.

Stupid mouth! That was not what she was supposed to

—

He captured her lips with his, and everything just melted. Thoughts, words, greenhouses.

It was just him and her and the heat of their mouths pressed together and she could never, ever get enough of it.

His lips were softer than she'd expected and he kissed her with a gentleness that was almost painful. His hands flattened against her back, pressing her closer to his chest.

Lian brought her arms to his shoulders, using her grip as leverage to kiss him harder. He growled, and she felt the low vibration through her chest.

She licked the seam of his lips, knowing she was playing with fire and not caring at all. He froze for a moment, then plunged his tongue into her mouth.

All the passion he'd obviously been holding back before crashed into her. His lips demanded more, his tongue sparring with hers, conquering.

Trying to, anyway. She hoped she was holding her own.

She let out a groan that would have mortified her with anyone else. With Nuar, she didn't care.

He growled again, his hands sliding around to her ample backside and lifting her. She wrapped her legs around his waist, settling against him, pressing her hips against his dick. He gasped and moved his lips to the skin beneath her ear, then raked those sharp teeth of his along her neck.

Goosebumps on her goosebumps on her goosebumps. Every inch of her skin stood at attention, begging for more.

"Lian," he said, a pleading note of his own in his voice. "Please…"

"Please what?" she asked, in a breathy voice she barely recognized.

"May I touch you?"

She actually let out a little laugh, but it turned into a gasp as he pressed his dick harder against her core. "What do you think you're doing now?"

"I wish to touch more of you. All of you."

"That sounds great."

Except they were in a public space. A wide-open public space.

"Wait," she said.

His fingers flexed against her ass and he held perfectly still. Very slowly, he pulled back to look at her.

God, those glowing eyes.

She licked her lips and his eyes glowed brighter, following the movement of her tongue.

I am so in over my head here.

"We should probably not be doing this here," she said.

A sharp voice cut right through the fog of her lust. "You think?"

Lian's gaze snapped over to the sidewalk in front of the greenhouse. To the group of people—the very large group of people—gathered and gawking at her making out with one of their new honored guests.

And, speaking of the Cygnians, four of them were among the group. The one in front, with his blue caveman beard, she recognized as Kral, the crown prince. He was sapphire blue, his hair a darker shade than his skin, and his eyes were glowing orange.

He did not look happy.

The warrior on his right had cobalt blue skin and yellow eyes. His dark blue hair hung in braids down his back, and he also sported a beard, but not nearly as cave-mannish as Kral's.

The Cygnian on Kral's left had sky-blue skin and hair so pale, it was almost white. His eyes were vibrant green and his slight smirk made her unsure if she liked him or wanted to smack him. Maybe both.

Another Cygnian with paler blue skin and whose eyes were almost lividly blue was regarding them with open curiosity. Only two of Kral's prism were missing. The ones with indigo and violet eyes—who would from that moment forward be the only Cygnians Lian could make eye contact with.

Vay, the Sadirian cultural liaison assigned to help aliens fit in, was standing on the other side of Kral's group. Her mouth was hanging open and her eyes were as wide as the flying saucers her people had arrived in.

Craig was in the back, one of his hands held over his face as he shook his head. His shoulders were jiggling, too, like he was laughing. The rat-bastard.

And in the very front of the group, her arms folded over her bright-green chest, was Azure, head of the Vegan contingent living in Harbor. The three-and-a-half-foot tall, emerald-green lizard person was somehow the most menacing of the group.

One of her brow ridges was arched high over her golden eyes as she regarded them, the bright sun glinting off of the metal bands of her super-high-tech exosuit.

"Oh shit," Lian said.

In her sibilant, raspy voice, Azure said, "Yes, 'oh shit' seems about right."

Chapter Five

"I am Azure, head of the Vegan contingent in Harbor," the small, reptilian lifeform said.

Nuar almost felt as though the planet's gravity had shifted. Was she truly a Vegan?

Her appearance matched the tales he'd heard. She was a bit over three feet tall, with a long tail that whipped about behind her, showing her agitation. Black stripes outlined in azure ran down her sides from along her spine and the silver bands of an exosuit wrapped around her wrists, biceps, arms, thighs, and ankles, all linked from a strip of material that ran down the middle of her back, leaving openings for her spines."

"We were told that there was an issue here," Azure said. She looked around at the greenhouse. "I would say that is something of an understatement."

Lian unwrapped her legs from Nuar's waist and slowly slid down his body. To his gratification, she didn't move away, but stayed at his side.

"When I told you we'd become a bit carried away, I was only talking about the greenhouse," Craig said. He waved one of his many hands toward Nuar and Lian. "I have nothing to do with this."

Nuar stepped forward. He was determined to show Lian that he could understand her concerns, that he could show support for them, and most of all, that he could help.

The more they interacted, the more his suspicions grew about his reactions to her. Their connection. That kiss had crystallized it—burned the truth into every fiber of his being.

She was his soulmate.

"The fault is mine," Nuar said. "Craig had kindly offered to help me return to the tour. I should not have allowed myself to be tempted to try my strength against his, knowing of this planet's…lack of density."

He glanced down at Lian, gratified to see her smirk at the end of his statement.

Kral did not look amused. His brow was furrowed in what Nuar knew to be tightly controlled fury. At least Lar, Dorn, and Bron seemed more confused than angered by the situation.

Once they knew the truth, they would be elated. Their prism shared their own form of soul bond. Now that Nuar had found his soulmate, they all had hope. Hope for a future with a female they could love.

Nuar couldn't believe he had found his soulmate on Earth. And if he had done so, others could as well. He just had to explain what was happening to Kral.

But perhaps not in front of Lian. Nuar needed time to figure out how best to approach her and win her affection.

Azure regarded him coldly for several moments. She narrowed her eyes and said, "This planet is precious to us, as is every Earthling living upon it. Had you injured one of them..." She angled her head to the side slightly. "Well, perhaps it is best not to think of such a scenario."

She kept staring at him, undoubtedly knowing he was envisioning just such a thing. Standing under Azure's scrutinizing stare and knowing what their technology was capable of, Nuar felt an unfamiliar sensation trickle down his spine.

Unease.

Surely not fear.

"I volunteer to correct the damage I've caused," Nuar said.

Azure's eyes widened. Kral's brow lowered further.

"It's only right that I do so." Nuar looked at Lian again. "I'm the one who broke this. I should be the one to fix it."

Lian smiled briefly, but then shook herself and forced her mouth back into a frown. He did his best not to laugh —and failed—which only made her scowl worse.

"First, I must speak with Kral." Nuar looked over at Kral and took in his glowing glare. "Or, rather, I think he must speak with me."

"Craig will begin work on repairs," Azure said.

"Me?" Craig huffed. "I have a nestling to consider."

"Barbara is perfectly capable of tending to your nestling." Azure added, rather pointedly, "And if necessary, Lian can watch over the child, as she so often does."

Vay bumped her shoulder against Craig's side. "I'll help."

Craig let out another sigh, then ambled into the greenhouse with Vay.

Nuar turned to Lian and said, "I need to begin work on creating replacements for the tools and structures we destroyed. I'll return as soon as I'm able. I swear to you, I will do everything in my power to restore the greenhouse."

"Sure." Her brow furrowed as if she didn't believe him.

He would win her faith, her heart, her soul.

With a low bow, he said, "By your leave."

Lar let out a sharp breath. Nuar could feel Kral's disapproval vibrating through the air surrounding them.

Nuar didn't care. As important as the prism was to him, Lian was even moreso.

She was everything.

He kept hunching over as a flurry of different emotions played across Lian's beautiful features. He longed to rise and bury his fingers in her dark hair, to trace the lines of her full lips, but held himself still.

"What are you doing?" she said.

"He's waiting for you to tell him he can go," Lar said.

She made a face. "Why? I mean, whatever. Go ahead."

Nuar stood and smiled at her. She frowned harder.

He turned to follow Kral and the others as they headed for the ship. Behind him, he heard Lian yell, "You are driving me freaking crazy!"

Nuar laughed and walked faster, knowing the sooner he could get this done, the sooner he could return to her with the backing and support of his prism. He glanced at her over his shoulder and waved, then leapt from the ground to the roof of one of the nearby buildings.

The look of surprise on her face was priceless. The expressions of Kral and the others when they landed next to him...not so much.

"You have much to explain," Lar said.

Nuar shook his head. "At the ship. Tarn and Rom need to hear this, too."

Kral surprised him by nodding his assent. Then he turned and started running along the roof. The rest of them followed, taking care when they launched themselves and when they landed that they didn't hurt the structures.

The town was so small, they reached the end of the buildings in moments. Rom was waiting for them. He looked at Kral's expression and started to say something, but Lar shook his head sharply. Rom wisely kept silent and turned back in the direction of the ship. With a giant leap, they cleared the last roof and landed on the ground.

None of them slowed their pace, sprinting across the field that stretched between the town and the spaceport disguised as an airfield a few miles distant. Dorn picked up speed, running ahead of Nuar.

With a laugh, Nuar pushed himself to run faster. He doubted he could overtake Dorn for long, but it would be fun to try.

The hangar housing their ship, the *Arrow*, appeared ahead of them. Dorn put on a burst of speed, then launched himself from the ground. Low gravity worlds could be fun.

Dorn landed right next to the hangar, then turned and smirked at Nuar. Nuar shook his head and laughed, choosing to remain on the ground for the last bit of the journey.

"I look forward to hearing your explanation," Kral said, slowing and then leading the way into the hangar.

The *Arrow* filled much of the generous space, hovering high off the ground. Light refracted off the sleek angles of its crystal hull, casting rainbows of color on the interior walls. Kral struck his wristbands together and a circular hatch opened on the underside of the ship.

One after another, they leapt the twenty feet up through the opening, landing in the ship. As soon as they were all aboard, Dorn secured the hatch. They followed Kral to the common room.

The other members of the prism spread out in the space. They knew when to expect a confrontation and Nuar had no doubt that was about to happen.

Rom leaned against the open archway for the corridor

that led to the cockpit. Tarn appeared in the archway that led to engineering and stood next to Bron. Lar and Dorn took up spots beside the corridor they were using to enter the room.

The moment Nuar and Kral entered the large, open area, Kral grabbed Nuar by the neck and spun him around, slamming him into the wall. Light rippled out from the impact through the milky-white crystal.

"What in the name of the Maker did you think you were doing?" Kral said. "I would expect this sort of recklessness from Rom perhaps, but not from you."

"Hey," Rom said. "What did he do, anyway? I was across the street, talking to one of the lovely Earthlings at that cafe."

"Aside from causing extensive damage to structures and equipment," Lar said. "He was rather indiscreetly... pursuing your preference of hobbies when we found him."

"Nice," Rom said.

"Don't encourage him." Kral tightened his grip and lifted Nuar so that his feet dangled above the ground. Nuar had never seen Kral so angry.

What was it about this planet? Why was Kral so intent on...

Understanding flooded Nuar's mind.

Kral had been ready to declare war on the Coalition and all their allies—including Earth. But then he'd met his first Earthling, Buddy, along with Buddy's dog, Pickles.

Kral had completely changed his mind.

He'd gone so far as to try to convince his parents, Queen Ehmach and King Korvin, to formally enter an alliance with Earth. Kral had begun the process when he met Buddy, and then insisted on visiting Earth with their prism to explore the possibility.

All after he'd heard Buddy's *sisters* talking to him over his communication device.

Kral snarled and lifted Nuar higher. "If Harbor decides we're too dangerous to be among Earthlings, they'll confine us to our ship or order us off the planet. With the Vegans backing them, we will have no choice but to comply."

"And then you'll never get to meet your soulmate," Nuar said.

Kral's eyes widened and his mouth dropped open, confirming Nuar's suspicions were true. But then, Kral snarled again and hurled Nuar across the room.

Nuar hit the wall with a bone-vibrating impact and bounced to the floor. He rolled to his feet. As he circled the space, Kral mirrored his movements.

"That's why we're on Earth, isn't it?" Nuar said. "You felt something when we heard the first broadcast from the planet. When Buddy shared his family's singing with us."

Kral charged him. Nuar didn't bother trying to duck out of the way, knowing his friend needed to let out his frustration and anger.

Nuar had only just met Lian and already he could barely stand to be apart from her. Kral had known of his soulmate's presence for months and he *still* hadn't been able to go to her.

Kral hit Nuar in the middle and lifted him from the ground. He carried Nuar across the room and slammed him into the wall again. Nuar clasped both hands together and brought them down on Kral's back. Kral grunted, but didn't let go.

"You're right," Nuar said. "If you felt something, you're right. She's here."

Kral finally released his hold, shoving away from Nuar. Pacing like a caged animal, Kral glowered at everyone around him. His hands curled and uncurled, claws extended. The plates along his spine had torn through his shirt and stood upright, sending out a steady pulse that signaled his readiness for battle.

Kral ripped the tattered fabric from his chest and threw it to the ground. "How can you be sure?"

"Because I've found mine," Nuar said. "Lian is my soulmate."

Kral stopped in his tracks. His eyes sparked even brighter, their orange like two blazing suns.

"Your soulmate?" Tarn said, stepping away from the wall. "Here?"

Nuar nodded. "I've found her. I'm sure of it. And she's an Earthling."

"Yeah, right." Rom laughed. "I've explored how compatible Cygnians are with other sentients, and as fun as it can be, I promise you the connection is purely physical."

Tarn scowled at Rom. Nuar could feel another fight brewing.

Of the prism, Tarn had been the most vocal about wanting to find his soulmate someday. Rom pretended to be fine with their situation, but they all knew he was anything but.

"You're wrong," Nuar said. "I held her in my arms. My hearts beat in unison for the first time in my life. I know she's my soulmate. In every atom of my being, I can feel it."

"This is ridiculous." Lar shook his head. "If we had soulmates, they would be Cygnian."

"Not that we have any chance to find a match among the few females remaining," Tarn said. There was a bitter edge to his voice. Nuar understood it all too well.

But now he had hope. Hope for all of them.

Lar stepped forward. "We all know there are too few Cygnian females remaining for us to hope to find our soulmates. We're already fortunate enough to be part of a prism. A full spectrum. The odds of us finding soulmates as well is infinitesimal."

"Our bond means that none of us will find a soulmate unless all of us can," Bron said. "That's the way it's always been with prisms. It's too much to hope for us to find seven matches when males outnumber females by more than a hundred-to-one on our Homeworld."

"That's what I'm trying to tell you," Nuar said. "If my soulmate is an Earthling, yours must be as well. They're here, on this planet."

Lar snorted. "Preposterous. We have pledged ourselves to our prism. Let that be enough."

"It *isn't* enough," Nuar yelled.

Everyone went still. He could feel their gazes on him. Their yearning. He knew it—had felt it every day since he realized that he would go through his life alone, perhaps resorting to fleeting pleasure or even marrying for companionship, but never finding the other half of his soul. The woman who made his hearts beat as one.

"You know I love you all like brothers," Nuar said. "I would die for each of you. But I would rather live. I would rather all of us live a full life. I want a mate. A partner to share my life with. I want *children*."

"Even if you feel something for a female here, it's impossible for you to breed with her," Bron said. "Cygnians are only compatible with Cygnians."

"Earth actually has children who need homes and loving families." That was part of the research on this planet he had paid close attention to. "Lian and I can adopt some. We can look into possibilities. The Vegans are here. If anyone could help us conceive, they could."

"Genetic manipulation?" Rom snorted. "Might as well take up with the Sadirians and join their Coalition. I'm sure they'd love to get more of our DNA and keep making hybrids in vats like they did to Kral's half-sister."

"Enough!" Kral shouted, his voice strong enough to make the walls vibrate with its echo. He stalked around the room, glaring at each of them in turn. Finally, he returned to Nuar.

"Our race is dying," Kral said. "There have barely been any children born on Cygnus-Prime in scores of Earth years. The children that we have are all male. My mother will have very difficult choices ahead of her. Even worse than the ones she's had to make up to this point."

"Kral," Nuar said, hearing the pleading in his own voice and not caring.

Kral placed his hands on Nuar's shoulders, gripping him tight.

"No one truly understands how the soul bond works," Kral said. "Not the bond among a prism, nor among the few soulmates that are left. But we do know that the connection transcends time and space. It is stronger than anything."

Bron shook his head. "That's the psychic connection. We can't say that the bond means we can have children—Cygnian children—with our mates if they aren't Cygnian, as much as our hearts might long for that."

"That doesn't mean there isn't a bond," Nuar said. "If

we can find our soulmates here, perhaps other Cygnians can as well. Earth is our future. It must be protected."

"Be reasonable, Nuar," Lar said, "We all felt a stirring at the Earthlings' singing, but it was just the way they were harmonizing their voices. The vibrations affected us on a physiological level. Perhaps the effect is lingering for you."

"Kral, you can't seriously believe this," Rom said.

"He can." Nuar gripped Kral's arms. "Because I'm right. He did feel something when he heard Buddy's sisters—one of them, anyway. Just as I felt something when I first heard Lian, angry as she was. And trust me, it is nothing—*nothing*—compared to what you will feel when you hold her in your arms."

Kral's grip tightened and his eyes flashed brightly. He nodded, then stepped away.

"I believe Nuar," Kral said. "I know how hard it is to let in hope after so long of facing down a future as bleak as we have been. But know this." He was quiet for a moment, again looking each warrior in the eye.

"I have felt my hearts stir toward unison," Kral said. "And it wasn't when the women sang. It was when the eldest sister, Becca, spoke."

The warriors were quiet and still. Tension filled the small space as they undoubtedly wrestled with daring to hope and yet wanting to protect themselves from more disappointment.

"That's why we're here," Tarn said. "You think Becca is your soulmate."

Kral nodded. "I wasn't sure. But after seeing Nuar and Lian together and hearing his words... I refuse to leave this planet until I've found out. The future of both of our planets hangs in the balance."

Chapter Six

Lian picked up her coffee and waved at the barista, then turned and headed for the exit. Nancy was right behind her, still chattering on and carrying her own coffee plus Olivia's. They joined Olivia on the sidewalk out front where she stood with Ed and Zorro, Olivia's huge black Newfoundland.

"Oh my god, I love your dress," Nancy said.

"Thank you." Olivia held out her skirt and did a little side-curtsy as best she could while holding the leashes of two enormous dogs. The pale yellow sundress looked amazing next to her brown skin. Then again, Olivia made everything she wore look amazing.

Nancy was the same way—with her perfectly styled blonde hair that matched her perfect figure for "pantsuits and power shoes," as she liked to call them. Lian would have felt under-dressed standing next to her besties if she cared about fashion at all.

Comfort was her motto. One of the perks of being an agricultural specialist working in a greenhouse every day was that she could get away with jeans and T-shirts.

Ed woofed as Lian took his leash. Nancy handed Olivia her coffee.

"Remind me again why you have such big dogs," Nancy said, trying to avoid getting tangled in Zorro's leash.

"Because if my dog was as small as yours, I'd have to start carrying a purse," Lian said.

As if she knew Lian was talking about her, Hazel, Nancy's long-haired, dappled teacup dachshund stuck her head out of Nancy's bag. Lian reached out and scratched behind the undeniably adorable dog's ears.

"It's also reassuring to have a big dog as a roommate when you live alone," Olivia added.

"I'd rather get myself a Cygnian." Nancy grinned. "Any advice there, Lian?"

"I advise you to shut up is what," Lian said.

Nancy laughed as they started down the sidewalk again. "I still can't believe I missed seeing you 'welcoming' the Cygnians."

"It was only the one," Lian grumbled, taking a sip of her too-hot coffee.

"I missed it, too," Olivia said. "And I was right across the street."

"If I hadn't had that stupid conference call, I would have met you guys for lunch like usual," Nancy said. "I hear Rom was in the cafe flirting with all the waitresses. Apparently, Bron is kind of brainy and inquisitive even though he's like a big, blue tank. Dorn is the 'strong and silent' type. He has kind of a more dangerous vibe. He's supposed to be their head of security. Do you know if he's their head of security?"

"You sound like you're talking about a boy band." Lian raised her voice an octave. "There's the smart one and the sporty one, but I like the bad boy best." Lian kicked her foot up behind her and plastered on a cheesy smile, batting her eyelashes for good measure.

"Shut up." Nancy bumped her shoulder against Lian's.

Olivia laughed, and said, "You probably wish you had a poster of all of them to hang above your bed."

"Come on, that's…" Nancy's gaze became a little unfocused and she paused in the middle of the sunny sidewalk.

Lian paused with her. "Nancy?"

"Hang on, I'm just visualizing that," Nancy said. "Oh wow, I think I actually do."

Lian laughed. "You're totally crushing on them."

"Says the girl who was caught making out with one of them in front of like almost every visiting foreign dignitary from another planet," Olivia said.

Lian felt her cheeks heat. "That was an accident."

Nancy made a little humming sound, then said, "That's not how I heard it."

Lian bumped her shoulder into Nancy's, a little harder than she anticipated. She also didn't realize Nancy was about to take a sip. Some of Nancy's coffee spilled.

"Hey," Nancy yelled.

"Sorry." Lian felt awful. "I didn't know you were about to take a drink."

"It's fine." Nancy wiped at her lip.

Olivia smirked and said, "Maybe Nuar can heal it for you like he did Lian's hand."

A wave of…something washed through Lian. Her chest constricted at the thought of Nuar paying attention to another woman's lips. *Any* other woman's lips. Even one of Lian's best friends.

"I was just kidding," Olivia said. "You don't have to give me the death stare."

"I'm sorry," Lian said. "Something is seriously wrong with me."

They had reached the front door of the library. Lian paused, wondering if she should keep going down the sidewalk toward the greenhouse or approach it through the attached building. Which would be less painful?

"Come on," Nancy said, hooking her elbow through Lian's.

Olivia leaned close enough that their shoulders brushed. "We've got you."

Lian's eyes started to burn. She blinked rapidly to clear her vision, then nodded.

"Okay," she said.

They headed down the sidewalk. Lian's heart beat

faster as more of the greenhouse came into view.

The energy walls were up. They were filled with shimmering opalescence, blocking her view of the inside. Usually, there was only a flickering, semi-transparent fizz filling the spaces between the support structures.

That was new. The Vegans had designed the walls so that people could always see into the greenhouse. What was going on in there?

The side door was open, at least. Ed gave a little 'woof,' then pulled her toward the entrance.

"Somebody's excited," Olivia said.

"Or maybe there's someone in there that he likes." Nancy winked at Lian.

Ed kept pulling. Lian let herself be half-dragged along, even though she didn't want to see this again.

"You guys should brace yourselves," Lian said. "This place is a disaster ar...e...a." Her voice trailed off as she crossed the threshold and stumbled a few steps within.

"Whoa," Olivia said.

Nancy joined Lian on her other side. "Oh, yeah. This place is a real mess."

"What is this?" Lian turned in a slow circle, taking everything in.

The plants that had been damaged were back. All of them, as if nothing had ever happened. Except that wasn't quite right.

The greenhouse looked better than before, mostly

courtesy of dozens of crystals hanging from the beams of the roof. They caught the sunshine that came in through the clear energy fields above and broke the light into thousands of rainbows that danced across every surface, lighting up the walls and rippling over their surface.

Her dad's bench had been replaced with a gorgeous slab of deep blue crystal. Smooth shards grew up behind it to form a back to lean on. It also caught the light, but seemed to hold it within, sparkling like a gigantic precious gem.

"This isn't possible," Lian said. "Everything was destroyed."

"It looks like Nuar fixed it," Olivia said.

"I'll say." Nancy headed straight for the bench. She ran her hand along the blunted edges of its back and said, "Oh my god. Is this sapphire?"

"It is." Nuar's voice boomed across the greenhouse. The sound of it reverberated through Lian, all the way to her bones.

Heat immediately flared deep in her belly and her skin rose in goosebumps again. She grumbled as she rubbed her arms, trying to calm herself down. Why did she always react this way to him?

Nuar strode over to them, a huge smile on his stupid, gorgeous face. His eyes were glowing red embers, focused intently on her, even though they were all standing in a magical wonderland.

A wonderland he had created. For her.

Presumably.

"Do you like it?" Nuar asked, still focused on Lian.

She crossed her arms. "It's okay."

"Okay?" Nancy said. "This place is a freaking paradise. And *is this really sapphire?*"

Nuar chuckled. "It's simple enough to grow. I started the seed crystal as soon as I could yesterday and worked on cultivating it in this form all night."

"All night, huh?" Olivia bumped her shoulder against Lian's again. "That was pretty sweet of you."

"He wouldn't have had to work on it all night if he hadn't destroyed the original bench in the first place," Lian said.

"Technically, Craig destroyed the bench," Nuar said.

Lian felt her eye twitch. "Only because you threw him at it."

"You threw Craig?" Nancy said.

Nuar shrugged. "Yeah."

"Craig the Lyrian." Nancy finally tore herself away from the bench to give Nuar her attention. "The seven foot tall, four-armed, space Sasquatch?"

He turned to Nancy and said, "I don't know what a Sasquatch is, but the rest describes Craig fairly well."

Nancy gave a high laugh and smiled. "I guess you're about as tall as he is, though."

She looked Nuar up and down as she approached him.

With every step Nancy took drawing closer to the Cygnian, Lian's goosebumps grew worse. Lian was grinding her teeth together so hard, her jaw hurt.

Why should she care if her friend flirted with the obnoxious blue alien? She hated him.

He wasn't good enough for Nancy. That was it.

But he had done *this* to the greenhouse. He'd made it right overnight.

Wait, that wasn't possible. If the plants could have been grown that quickly, the Vegans would have done it from the start. Azure was very clear that there were limits to what they could do, and speeding the plants' growth too much wasn't necessarily a good thing.

"How did you fix the plants?" Lian asked.

"Ah, yes." Nuar had the decency to look sheepish. "The plants. I actually didn't fix them. I used imagery collected over the last few weeks to overlay a hologram that makes the greenhouse look as it did before yesterday. That way, people can enjoy it just as much while the plants regrow."

"You mean this is all an illusion?" Lian asked.

Nuar nodded. "Except the bench. The bench is real."

"Show me," Lian said.

Nuar sighed, then struck his wristbands together. They made a sound kind of like a Tibetan signing bowl, drawn out by a low humming sound Nuar made himself.

She felt it like a shockwave, intensifying that weird

reaction she always had to his voice. She was just about to tell him to stop when he did so on his own.

"Oh no," Olivia said.

Lian looked around at what she'd expected to see. Except maybe not as bad.

The plants were definitely different. But they'd been pruned back past the breakage points. The ones that had been trampled were removed, and smooth, loose earth remained in their place, ready for something new to be planted.

A few of the taller plants had been grafted back together where their trunks had been snapped. Sparkling bands held them in place.

"It's not as easy to heal a plant," Nuar said. "I was with Azure and Craig most of the night, tending to the flora when I wasn't making trips back to the *Arrow* to work on the bench. We all did as much as we could, but Craig and I are both from planets nearly devoid of plant life. Our experience with them is limited."

"You don't have plants on your homeworld?" Lian felt the idea of it like a gut-punch. "How do you survive? What do you eat?"

"The plants that we do have are nutritious lichens that grow in cave systems on Cygnus-Prime," Nuar said. "And we also hunt animals who feed on the crystals that make up much of our homeworld."

"That sounds so weird," Nancy said.

"No weirder than our world probably is to them," Olivia said.

Nuar didn't comment on their exchange. Instead, he said, "Azure helped us adapt our technologies to assist her with tending the plants. I could do more than Craig, but he helped with the digging and pruning." Nuar lifted his arms and wiggled his fingers. "He's handy that way."

Lian almost snorted. She managed to stifle it.

Nuar cleared his throat. "Craig said you'd find that funny."

"Too soon," Olivia said.

"Leave it like this," Lian said. "I won't trick people into thinking everything's okay when it's not."

She might have emphasized the last part more than she intended. Nuar winced. Part of her wanted to comfort him.

Dammit.

He had done a lot to make up for the harm he'd caused. He and Craig. She had to remember to be mad at both of them.

It was easier to be mad at Nuar. She didn't know him as well. Then again, the more she got to know him, the more she was starting to like him.

Double-dammit.

"You really should leave it like this," Olivia said. "People need to know where things are. It'd be unsettling for them to try to touch a plant and have their hand pass through it. I'm assuming their hand would pass through it?"

Nuar nodded. "Yes. Our holographic technology is the most advanced in the galaxy, but even we can't add substance to imagery."

"Can you add AC to it?" Nancy asked. "Because it's freaking muggy in here."

Nuar cocked his head to the side. "AC?"

"Air conditioning," Lian said. "We usually keep the walls open to let in a breeze."

"I can fix that." His face lit up with a dazzling smile.

It should be illegal to be that hot.

He struck his wristbands together again. Lian knew it was coming this time and was able to keep her poker face as her belly flooded with heat again.

The walls fizzed and vanished. A breeze immediately swept through the place.

"That's so much better," Nancy said, closing her eyes. "But I need to get to work anyway. See you guys later."

She quickly hugged Olivia and Lian, then headed outside, casting one last smile at Lian, along with a mocking wave over her shoulder.

Olivia patted Zorro's head. "We need to get the dogs inside where it's cooler."

"Allow me." Nuar hurried to the door to the library and opened it.

Olivia followed him with Zorro at her side. She looked back at Lian and smirked as she entered the building.

Ugh, Lian was never going to hear the end of this.

Nuar was still holding the door open. Ed started pulling Lian toward it. She scowled at the Cygnian as she passed.

Okay, she tried to scowl at him.

He *had* done a really good job with the greenhouse. And he'd made that stunning bench and added the crystals, making the incredible rainbow display.

Sure, the plants had been messed up, but most had been saved. They would grow back. The damage he'd caused them wasn't irreversible.

Mostly.

"Thanks," she mumbled as she passed him.

She wasn't sure if she was talking about holding the door or everything he'd done to make things right, but the way his expression brightened made her not really care. A fluttery feeling rose in her stomach. One that was nearly impossible to ignore.

Triple-dammit.

Chapter Seven

Nuar followed Lian and her friends into the data repository known as a library. He wasn't quite sure how the building worked. There didn't seem to be any data crystals in the site—just shelves full of strange rectangular blocks that reminded him of the brick he'd pulverized the day before.

He was very careful not to touch anything.

As soon as they entered the space, both Lian and Olivia removed the leads attached to collars placed around their mounts' necks. He wondered what kind of animals they were, but loved that they were used as steeds for children.

"Nuar, would you mind filling up Ed and Zorro's dishes with fresh water?" Olivia asked. "They must be thirsty after walking around in that heat."

"I'm happy to help, if you'll instruct me on what to do," he said.

"You know what? I really need to get started reshelving these books." Olivia turned to Lian, and said, "You can help him, right?"

Lian grimaced at her friend, then stomped past Nuar.

Olivia winked at him and smiled. He wasn't sure what that meant, but he did the same back. Perhaps somewhat awkwardly, based on Olivia's laughter as he turned to follow Lian.

Lian led him to a low basin with water transfer pipes. Nuar recognized them from working with Craig and Azure the night before.

"The bowls are there." Lian nodded to the floor, where two large dishes sat on a bright yellow rubber mat. One was red and one was black. Nuar lifted each dish, examining them more closely.

The red dish had a line drawing of an animal that looked very similar to Ed. It was lying down with its eyes closed and for some reason several letter 'Z's were emanating from its head. The black dish had a drawing of a silver stick with a hilt. It looked as though the stick had been used to draw another letter 'Z'.

Nuar had learned that the huge black animal's name was Zorro. Perhaps Ed's dish was supposed to depict him dreaming of his furry friend?

Strange.

"Rinse them out first," Lian said, bending over to turn on the water.

Nuar smiled as the liquid poured into the basin. He set the dishes on its rim, then plunged his hands into the water.

"It's cold," he said, laughing.

"Please tell me you've seen a sink before," Lian said. "Don't they have water where you're from?"

"Not like this." Nuar was spellbound by the way the light caught in the water. "It's almost like liquid crystal."

"Where do you get water on your planet? Or do you not need to drink?"

It pleased him that she was taking an interest in his people—in him.

"The same lichen we use for much of our food provides water. If we press it, the water is released. Usually, we push our hands against it and drink from our palms, but we don't need to do so often."

He cupped his hand and filled it, then lifted it to his mouth to drink. Her scowl deepened when he looked up at her, laughing.

"That's not how…" Lian shook her head and sighed.

She reached past him to pick up the bowls, her arm brushing his and her body close. The plates along his spine started to rise.

Now was not the time. Olivia was still nearby, as well as Ed and Zorro. Aside from that, he wasn't sure how Lian would react to seeing this aspect of him.

The differences in his anatomy when compared to a human male were…significant. Would they be too alien for her?

She hadn't seemed to mind his red eyes or blue skin or the fact that he was almost two feet taller than her. That didn't mean she would be so accepting of everything else.

Lian rinsed the bowls quickly, then held them beneath the water to catch it. As soon as she had filled the first, he reached for it.

"Please, let me," he said. "I'm supposed to be learning, not letting you do my work for me."

She cast that familiar scowl at him, but handed him the dish. He smiled in return, then placed it back where he'd found it on the floor.

Ed immediately came over to drink. The poor beast seemed very thirsty.

Nuar hurriedly took the next bowl and set it down, assuming Zorro would be thirsty as well. Sure enough, the moment the bowl touched the ground, the large animal joined Ed.

They looked as though they might be a similar species. Their shape and size were the same, and they had soft, shaggy fur covering their bodies. But Zorro was all black, and Ed was a mix of reddish-brown and white. His cranial shape and muzzle were also a bit different.

"Sorry the sink is so low," Lian said. "This is the kids' section of the library."

"There are children here?" Nuar turned around, quickly scanning the area.

He saw bright drawings and artwork on the walls in the prismatic colors he was accustomed to seeing on Cygnus-Prime. While the pictures showed small humans in various activities, he didn't see any actual children.

"Settle down," Lian said. "The library doesn't open for another hour. Kids usually only show up on the weekends, anyway."

"Oh." Nuar's hearts ached with disappointment. He hadn't seen a child since he had been one himself.

"I'm guessing you really like kids," Lian said.

"I love children. I would have at least a dozen if I could."

Lian shook her head. "That's a lot to ask of a woman."

"I plan to adopt," he said.

"Oh." She looked vaguely confused and a bit unsettled. "That's nice. You have somebody back home, then."

"No." He shook his head vigorously and reached for her, only remembering at the last minute that he needed to ask first. The wariness in her eyes made him doubt she'd say yes. "I don't. I just… It's unlikely that I'm capable of fathering children."

"Oh, damn," she said, her eyes widening. "I'm sorry. Maybe the Vegans can help you."

"Perhaps they can." He smiled, actually considering the thought.

If the Vegans could help him, then he and Lian *could* have children of their own. Surely the other members of his prism would understand him seeking genetic assistance if it meant that his people could go on.

He also loved the idea of sharing their home with

children who needed a family. With the help of the Vegans, they might be able to do both.

"With Cygnian technology, pregnancies would be safe and easy," Nuar said, eager to warm her to the idea. "I've studied some of Earth's medical techniques in regard to children. There is…room for improvement."

"I imagine so." Lian actually smiled.

The sight about undid him. But she wasn't looking at him, she was gazing at the wall, her eyes unfocused.

"The hospital is my favorite new addition to Harbor," she said. "We used to have to drive to other towns to get decent medical care. The Vegans and Antareans built this wonderful facility that tends to all kinds of sentients. I helped with the integration of plants in the environment and learned about the amazing things they can do there. I used to be scared about having kids, but now, not so much."

The thought of her having children with someone else made his spine plates stiffen. He wanted to put his fist through the wall.

Lian looked up at him, her cheeks pink. The way she stared, he almost dared to hope that she was imagining having children with him.

"We should um…wash our hands," Lian said. She turned away from him quickly, but not before he saw another of those cautious smiles of hers.

Hope bloomed in him.

"Why do we need to wash our hands?" he asked, eager to learn more of her world.

She arched an eyebrow at him. "I don't know about you, but I'd rather make sure I don't have Ed's spit on my hands if I want to eat a brownie or something."

Ed's spit... Nuar glanced down at the furry beast, who was sitting on his haunches and looking up at him, his mouth open and tongue lolling out.

There was quite a bit of drool involved.

She had a point. Nuar struck his wristbands together and hummed the note that activated their decontamination waves. Light flowed over his hands, incinerating any unwanted bacteria or foreign substances.

Lian scowled at him as she pushed on a black box that protruded from the wall. A thick foam squirted out of it onto her palm. She rubbed the foam between her hands for a few moments, then rinsed them under the water.

"What is that supposed to accomplish?" Nuar asked.

"Soap and water is how we kill germs here on Earth." She gestured to his wristbands and said, "We don't all have access to your magic technology that probably keeps your hands clean and smelling minty fresh."

"Minty..."

"You know what I mean," she snapped.

He laughed again, despite himself. "I really don't."

"Forget it."

She reached to turn off the water, but he put his hand

on the activation lever to stop her. Her hand landed on his. Rather than jerk away, she left it there. Her eyes widened and her lips parted.

That was a good sign.

"Please," Nuar said. "I want to learn."

She took her hand away and nodded. Her voice had a rasp to it when she spoke.

"Fine, then. The soap is there." She pointed at the black box. "Press this to dispense some. Then lather up your hands for a while and rinse them."

He did as she instructed, enjoying the way she watched his movements. The intensity of her gaze encouraged him that she was feeling the same pull to him that he was to her. He lingered as he rinsed the soap from his hands.

She waved her hand in front of a larger, metal box and paper flowed out of it. She took two sheets and handed him one. He emulated her movements as she used the one she kept to dry her hands.

"The Vegans are working with us on technology that will be better at killing germs and even removing dirt," Lian said, "but we don't want to make the changes too fast. Harbor is supposed to be where we try out new systems that we can spread across the planet. If we change too much, too fast, it could cause problems."

"The rest of the populace might catch on that the technology is extra-terrestrial in origins?"

"Not just that. We want to do things on our own. With

help, of course, but we don't want to just take handouts. We've heard too many horror stories of what happened to planets that joined the Coalition and became dependent on their tech when the High Council was still in charge."

His spine plates started to vibrate, but for a much less pleasant reason. He angled his body to make sure his back was out of her sight and tried to keep them clamped down.

"The High Council may have been behind many of the crimes against other sentients, but Sadirians carried out those orders," Nuar said. "They should be held accountable."

"It's not that simple. From what I understand, a huge portion of their population was drugged and subjected to mental programming. Most of the time, they didn't even know their minds were being manipulated." She shook her head. "It's messed up."

"You have sympathy for Sadirians."

"Hell yeah, I do. I live with them. They're my neighbors. Clara, the mayor's bondmate or wife or whatever you want to call it, was among the Sadirians who had their emotions suppressed in one of the High Council's experiments. She's…kinda weird, but she's nice enough. She's trying hard to fit in. They all are."

Nuar held his silence, trying to calm his emotions.

"What is it?" she asked, stepping a bit closer. Her voice was gentler than he'd ever heard it before. "What did they do to you?"

"Not me," he said. "Kral's sister, Sorca. Somehow, the High Council convinced Queen Ehmach and King Korvin to provide the High Council with Cygnian DNA. They wouldn't ask any of their subjects to make such a sacrifice, so they provided their own."

"I'm sure they had a good reason," Lian said.

"If they did, it's not one I can comprehend." Nuar shook his head. "According to their agreement, the High Council was only supposed to create one Sadirian-Cygnian hybrid soldier."

"And they didn't?"

"As with everything the High Council did, they twisted it to suit their purpose. They only created Sorca, but they made multiple copies of her."

"Why would they do that?"

"We don't know. All we know is that they were experimenting on her to test her limits and improve upon her design," Nuar said, disdain heavy in his voice. "I've read through all the data we could retrieve and it's horrifying what they subjected her to."

"I'm sorry."

He nodded briefly, unsure what to say, yet compelled to continue. He needed Lian to understand why the Cygnians could never ally themselves with the Coalition, even now that the High Council had been destroyed.

"They only had one version of Sorca active at a time," Nuar said. "Sadirians used the mental programming techniques you spoke of to imprint her memories on each successive body. She would periodically have her memories downloaded at secret facilities. Then they would send her into situations they doubted she would survive."

"Oh my god."

"Most of the time, she didn't. They would activate another clone and imprint her latest memories on that body. When she did return unexpectedly, they would destroy all of the clones they had in stasis and create a new batch based on the 'improved version.'"

"Nuar..."

His eyes blurred strangely. The plates on his back were clamped against his spine as he spoke, instead of standing on end and vibrating, warning others of his readiness for battle.

"She died hundreds of times," he said. "And she knew. The entire time this was going on, she knew. They didn't even give her the comfort of thinking that she was only living one life. That her life as it was—her individual life —had value."

Lian let out a shaky breath and shook her head. "Look, I'm pissed as hell on your behalf. That is awful and I'm even more glad that the High Council was wiped out. But you can't go around hating all Sadirians because of what a few of them did."

Nuar let out a strange, strangled laugh. "Can't I?"

"Not if you're going to stay in Harbor. Not if Cygnians

are going to be friends with Earth. Not if… Not if you're going to be friends with me."

Chapter Eight

Lian felt sick to her stomach after hearing Nuar's story. She could absolutely understand why he hated Sadirians. Kral probably hated them even more. But then why were they here on Earth?

She also understood why the Coalition wanted to be allies with Earthlings. They needed resources and new homes for their people when their battles didn't go well—which seemed to be happening a disturbing amount of the time.

From what Lian had learned, Earth had nothing to offer the Cygnians in terms of resources they might need. There had to be something drawing them to her planet, though. She grew uneasy wondering what it might be.

"How are you guys doing over here?" Olivia appeared around one of the shelves a few seconds after speaking. She probably thought Lian and Nuar were making out again and wanted to warn them that she was coming.

"Well enough," Nuar said, his smile somewhat strained.

Lian kept her response to a muted, "Fine."

"That's great," Olivia said, stopping close to them. "I still have a lot of reshelving to do, and I'm sure you both have work in the greenhouse. You can leave the dogs with me."

"Dogs?" Nuar's face lit up. He looked all around him, almost as excited as he'd been when Lian mentioned kids.

Warmth blossomed in her chest as she remembered his expression. She needed to get this infatuation or whatever it was out of her system. If only she knew how.

"I don't see any dogs." The disappointment on Nuar's face would have been heart-wrenching if he hadn't been looking in the direction of Ed and Zorro.

"They're right there," Lian said, gesturing to the dogs.

"What, Ed and Zorro?" Nuar laughed. "Don't be ridiculous. Those aren't dogs."

"Oh my god, could you be any more condescending?" Lian said.

"I didn't mean to be," he said.

"Well then, you must be a natural," Lian snapped.

Olivia pulled her lips between her teeth and pinched them there. She let out a little snorting laugh through her nose, though.

"I'll deal with you later," Lian said.

At that, Olivia did burst out laughing. She leaned in and hugged Lian, earning a growl.

"Are you sure it's safe to approach her at the moment?" Nuar asked.

"Of course it is," Olivia said. "Lian only bites with her words."

Lian glared at Olivia.

"And her glare." Olivia stepped away from Lian and grasped Nuar's elbow. "Come on, I have some books that might help."

Why did she have to touch him to show him the books? She could just point.

Olivia looked back at Lian over her shoulder, one eyebrow arched.

Dammit, she was doing it to bait Lian. Well, the joke was on Olivia, because Lian wasn't falling for it. She crossed her arms and followed them deeper into the kid's section.

"Let's see, I think this one will do." Olivia pulled out a big picture book that had a motley group of dogs on the cover. She opened the book and started pointing at pictures. "These are all different types of dogs."

"That's impossible," Nuar said. "They have so many different shapes and sizes and— Pickles!"

Lian did a double-take. What kind of a dog had pickles?

Nuar pointed at a picture of a Pomeranian and said, "This is Pickles! My Earth-friend Buddy has one of these. *This* is a dog."

"So are all of these other breeds," Olivia said.

"How did you create such diversity in their

appearances?" he asked. "The level of genetic manipulation required is well beyond Earth's technology."

"We did it the old fashioned way," Lian said. When he looked at her quizzically, she added, "Selective breeding over thousands and thousands of years."

He looked from the book back to Ed and Zorro, who were splayed out on the cool floor, dissipating heat. Summer was not their best season.

"Incredible." He gestured toward the book and said, "May I?"

"Sure." Olivia handed it over.

"What is this?" he asked.

Lian scooted closer so she could see whatever was on the page. It was still the same picture of a Pomeranian.

"That breed is called a Pomeranian," Lian said.

"But what is..." He lifted the book and looked underneath it, then lowered it and carefully angled it from side to side.

"What, you mean the book?" Lian asked.

"Book," he repeated. "My translation session describes a book as a static source of data."

"I suppose you could say that," Olivia said. "I like to think of them as infinite possibilities."

Nuar stared at her blankly.

"Here, let me show you." She took the book from him and put it back on the shelf, then led him to a different section of the library.

Lian followed along. Because she was curious. Not because she felt some kind of weird pull toward Nuar, almost like they were connected somehow and—

Ugh, just stop.

"We have books for all ages and skill levels here." Olivia took a book from the shelf and handed it to Nuar. "Just be careful not to tear the pages."

He looked at her expectantly and she showed him how to open the book and turn the page. He took over, quickly leafing through it.

"Do you need a book with more pictures?" Lian said.

Olivia glared at her. "Hey."

Nuar didn't seem to mind. Then again, he might not have picked up on the jab.

"This is full of inaccuracies," he said.

"There's no way you can read that fast," Lian said.

"I can." He lifted the book for her to see. "But there is no way that faster than light travel could happen this way."

"These books are fiction," Olivia said.

"Fiction," he said. "My language doesn't have a corollary."

"You've got to be kidding," Lian said. "You don't have stories on your world?"

"Of course we have stories," he said. "That's how we preserve our history. We use reprogrammable data crystals instead of books, though."

Olivia broke out her 'patiently explaining' voice. "We

have stories like that, too. We call them nonfiction or histories. But on Earth, we also enjoy making up stories. Thinking about things that could be, but aren't."

"What's the point of that?" he asked.

"Fiction helps us escape reality," Olivia said. "Or learn to handle it better—sometimes at the same time. We can experience things through other people's perspectives. It helps us learn empathy."

"There is no escaping from reality," he said. "That's what makes it...reality."

"Please." Lian rolled her eyes. "What do you guys do for fun?"

Without hesitating he said, "We practice our fighting skills and challenge each other to feats of prowess."

"That explains a lot," she said, her voice thick with sarcasm.

"Hey guys," Olivia called from...somewhere across the library. When had she left? "I just remembered that I have a...thing. An errand I really need to run right now. You don't mind watching the library for me, right? We open in about an hour and the dogs are napping. I'll be back in time to open, but not before. Thanks!"

Lian didn't even have a chance to reply before she heard the door close. She looked back at Nuar, blithely reading his book, then past him at the shelves surrounding them. Her cheeks suddenly started burning.

They were in the Sci-fi Romance section.

"Oh, I'm going to get her for this," Lian said.

Nuar let out a laugh at something in the text. "This is completely unbelievable. Not even a Scorpiian could assume the form of the Der'Eghon, and Scorpiians are the greatest shapeshifters in the galaxy."

"Yeah, we've all seen the Department of Homeworld Security PSA videos warning us about Dean, the Scorpiian that was hanging around Harbor a few months back, but —" She noticed that the book he was reading had a picture of a giant dragon on the cover, as well as a spaceship and a couple embracing. "Wait, there are alien dragons out there? Dragons are real?"

"Dragons," he repeated, with the same thoughtful expression as when he'd said the other words that were new to him. "I suppose that's a good enough transliteration of their name."

"Space dragons," Lian said.

Nuar shrugged. "There are sentients in the Pollux system in the constellation you call Gemini who have forms similar to these, but they can't shapeshift. The mass variations alone..." He shook his head. "They also can't leave their planet. Or rather, they choose not to. Can you imagine the size of ship they would need to house even a single Der'Eghon, let alone a crew?"

She liked dragon shifter romances. Olivia and Nancy were the ones into blue aliens. Then again, checking out Nuar's physique as he turned back to his book, Lian could definitely see the appeal.

When he wasn't putting his big blue foot in his mouth.

He had broad shoulders and a narrow waist. The T-shirt he was wearing was tucked in, so she had a magnificent view of his equally magnificent ass.

The sleeves weren't actually big enough to fit his huge biceps properly. The fabric was stretched taut over them. Actually, now that she was looking closer, the T-shirt was stretched tight just about everywhere. So were his jeans.

She remembered that impressive bulge pressing against her, and heat detonated in her core. Not a gentle warmth. Not an uncoiling or whatever. A full-on nuclear blast.

She licked her lips, her mouth going dry. What was it about this guy?

As she watched, something along his spine moved beneath his shirt. She froze, mesmerized.

Slowly, the fabric rose as a row of short spines stood up in a line down the center of his back. She could tell they weren't sharp—otherwise they would have torn right through the material. They weren't pointy either. The shape looked more like a stegosaurus's than a Vegan's, from the straining fabric of his shirt.

His arms lowered a bit, his eyes glowing so bright, the page was bathed in red light. She looked over to see what he was reading.

Oh shit.

It was one of *those* scenes.

Chapter Nine

Those spines brought new meaning to "hard-on." They were also weirdly appealing. Lian wished she could see what they looked like without his shirt on.

"Calm down," she said. "It's fiction, remember?"

She raised her arm to...she wasn't sure what she'd intended. But she ended up cautiously running her hand down his spines as if she could smooth them back to his body.

Nuar groaned, his knees almost buckling. He reached out and steadied himself against the shelf.

Oh wow, were his spines *really* like a hard-on? The thought hit her with another heat blast, her core starting to throb.

She pulled her hand back quickly. "Sorry, I should have asked first."

He kept his grip on the shelf, so tight she wondered that the material didn't splinter. The books in front of him were bathed in the red light of his gaze.

"You have my permission to touch me whenever and wherever you wish." The rasp to his voice was like velvet tracing over her skin.

She bit her lower lip, her fingers twitching with the need to touch him. Was she really going to do this?

She wasn't sure. At least, not in her head. Her hand was already reaching for his back again.

Gently, she traced her fingertips over the edges of his spines. His eyes rolled shut and he groaned. He set down the book he'd been holding and grabbed onto the shelf with both hands.

Damn, how was this so hot? It should be weird, not hot.

Then again, having a seven-foot tall, red-eyed, blue alien completely at her mercy was kind of... Okay, it was super hot.

Out of curiosity, she ran her other hand along his back, to see if he was sensitive all over or just on his spines. The touch seemed to relax him a bit and he let out a breath. She, on the other hand, nearly erupted again.

Holy crap, the muscles on this guy!

She explored the firm curves of his lats, then let her fingers trail down to his narrow waist. She really, *really* wanted to know what other surprises he might have in store for her.

This was doing nothing for her infatuation with him. What was that saying? *The only way out is through?*

Nuar was catching his breath. She wasn't okay with that. With a smile, she ran her hand along his spines—this time, with a firmer touch.

Nuar threw his head back and groaned again. She wasn't quite sure, but it looked like his fingers were actually sinking into the "indestructible" Vegan material.

"Lian…" he pleaded.

Shit, this was a power rush.

But was she abusing it? She didn't want to push him into something he didn't want.

Then again, how the hell could she push him into anything? He could easily overpower her.

The thought should have been scary, but it wasn't at all. He'd been nothing but gentle with her, even when she'd broken her hand trying to punch his lights out. Except for when he'd held onto her wrist—behavior he'd immediately corrected when she told him to.

She didn't want to lead him on. But that probably wasn't a possibility, either. Everybody knew the Cygnians were just visiting. She doubted they would stick around long.

He seemed willing to indulge her curiosity. And she was pretty sure he'd be up for indulging a little of his own.

The idea of his hands exploring her set her off again. But this was her turn, and she wanted to see how much she could get away with.

She stepped closer to him, sliding her hands around to his stomach. So many abs. And his front felt as good as his back.

She let her hands explore his chest, smoothing them

over his pecs and then back down over his stomach. If only he didn't have the damn shirt on.

At first, it was a little awkward working around the row of spines, but when she realized they weren't dangerous, she leaned against them.

The were vibrating.

What the hell?

Now that she was closer, she could hear a low humming sound. Actually, she could feel it more clearly than anything.

The movement sent shivers through her body, resonating all the way to her bones. The throbbing in her core intensified as she pressed against his back. It made her wonder what other parts of him could do. She lowered her hands to the waistband of his jeans.

Once more, she asked herself if she was really doing this. Nuar choose that moment to let out another low moan as her fingers slipped across his stomach just beneath the waistband of his jeans.

Yeah, she was doing this, all right.

Olivia was gone, the library was locked up, the dogs were asleep in another section, and they were very, very close to Lian's office—which had a couch covered in blankets that Lian had never taken home after the winter.

She stroked her hand over the front of his jeans, causing him to gasp and jerk against the shelves. Something crunched.

They could fix it later. Maybe Nuar would replace it with a solid-sapphire shelf.

Lian undid the button of his fly and spread his jeans open, giving herself access to what was inside.

Boxer-briefs. Okay, she could work with that.

She slid her hand deeper, stroking him through the soft fabric and—

Oh my god! Are those ridges?

Nuar pressed back against her gently. His chest heaved with each breath.

She lifted the waistband of his boxer-briefs, unable to hold back her curiosity or the deeper, primal need to touch more of him.

Reaching in, she wrapped her hand around his shaft. As much as she could, anyway. How was she ever going to manage *that?*

She would figure it out.

He let out another groan as she pulled her hand up along his dick. Definitely ridged, but not in a scary way. Damn, that would feel good sliding into her.

She needed him naked. Immediately.

"Nuar."

"Yes?"

She'd never heard so much need in a single word.

"Follow me," she said.

It took an act of will to release him, but the promise of so much more helped her manage. She didn't bother to redo his jeans, either. She wanted them gone as soon as possible.

She'd never been happier that her office was close to the Sci-fi Romance section. She hurried through the open door, and closed it the moment he crossed inside.

"What is this place?" he asked, glancing around.

"My office. Now get naked."

"What?"

Had she been misreading him? Had he just been so swept away by the story he'd been reading that he'd been caught up in the moment and she'd unintentionally taken advantage?

That would be beyond awkward.

"I'm sorry, I thought you wanted—" she began.

He took a step forward, reaching for her, but not touching her.

"I do," he said. "I want you. I want more of what you were doing out there. I want everything you have to offer me."

"Oh."

Damn.

Before she could talk herself out of it, Lian threw herself at Nuar, wrapping her arms around his neck and pulling herself up to kiss him. He bent down, pressing his lips against hers.

She wished he would pick her up again. With how he was hunching over, he was going to hurt his back. At least, a human guy would.

But he wasn't a human guy. Point in case, he was holding his hands out next to her sides and moving them weirdly.

She broke off the kiss. "What are you doing?"

In a pained voice, he said, "Not touching you."

"Oh."

"Please, may I touch you?" he asked.

As much as she longed to feel his strong hands on her, she wasn't quite ready for him to do that, yet. Once he did, she knew things would progress rapidly, and she wasn't done exploring him.

"No," she said.

He actually winced. She felt bad for him, until she thought about what she had planned.

"Take off your shirt," she said, backing away just enough to give him space to do so.

He looked a bit hopeful, then pulled his shirt over his head and tossed it on her small couch. Looking at it and then him... Yeah, they'd have to pull the blankets onto the floor or something.

That chest, though...

The blue covering his chest gleamed, catching and refracting the light almost as if his skin itself were crystal. His eyes glowed brighter as she looked at him.

She really wished they had more than an hour.

Forcing herself to look calm, she walked around behind

him to get a better look at those dinosaur spine plates. They ran from the base of his neck down to the waistband of his jeans, with larger plates toward the center of his back, and smaller ones at the top and bottom of the row. The largest was about twice the size of her palm.

They were broader than she'd expected and midnight blue. She could see little segments in each one that seemed like some sort of support structure. It looked like they would cover his vertebrae when they were flat against his skin. Maybe they were some kind of extra body armor?

Very cool.

She had other things she wanted to see, but while she was back there, she couldn't resist touching them.

His spine plates quivered beneath her fingers, the vibration intensifying. She had expected them to be hard—which they were—but they were also warm and their texture was velvety.

Nuar didn't groan this time. He stood unnaturally still, his spine completely straight. She leaned forward so she could see his face. His eyes were pinched shut and the muscles on his jaw stood out tensely.

Nice.

She dropped down and unlaced his boots for him. When she looked up again, he was staring at her.

"Shoes off," she said. She held them on the ground as he pulled his feet from them, then she stood and crossed her arms. "Now the rest of it."

He quickly stripped off his socks, then hooked his thumbs in the waistband of his boxer-briefs and pushed them down along with his jeans. When he stood, her jaw dropped open.

It wasn't the thick blue erection jutting at her that had her absolutely speechless. It was that there were two of them.

How had she not felt that earlier?

"Oh my god," she said.

Nuar looked taken aback.

"In a good way," she added quickly. "A very good way." She swallowed hard. "Those are... That's... Really something. Two somethings."

"It's how we are," he said.

She pulled her gaze away from his groin, taking in his muscular thighs, ripped abs, and flawless physique.

"And I'd say you're about perfect," she said, because admitting he *was* perfect might go to his head.

After this, she was definitely going to have a thing for blue aliens.

A little twinge hit her. Thinking about "after Nuar" was...troubling. She shook the thought away and focused on the moment. If they didn't have unlimited time, she wanted to use what they had properly.

He smiled as she walked up to him. The smile faded as she dropped to her knees.

Was that confusion? Did that mean they didn't do this

kind of thing on his planet?

Well, she was either about to create an interplanetary incident or make a radical shift in their bedroom activities.

Two. Oh, I can have some fun with this.

His dicks were stacked one on top of the other instead of being side-by-side. She gripped them both and gave them long strokes.

Nuar groaned again. He didn't have a bookshelf to destroy, so she hoped he could keep his balance—and keep his hands to himself.

This might be a little tricky...

She kept her strokes on the top dick going, then clasped the bottom one and ran her tongue along its crown. Nuar made an altogether new sound, a gasping groan that was pure pleasure. She would have smirked if she could, but her mouth was busy.

She licked his shaft, working it with her hand as well since *damn* there was a lot of it. By the time she was done, he would never, ever forget his time on Earth.

Another of those twinges hit her.

Focus.

She wrapped her lips around as much of his crown as she could manage, swirling it with her tongue and sucking hard. Nuar gasped again. He reached for her head, but curled his hands into fists before touching her.

Were those *claws* she'd caught a glimpse of? Her skin rose in goosebumps.

She pressed his top dick against his stomach and pinned it there so she could give her full attention to the one in her mouth. It was already starting to pulse. The other wasn't, which was a very good sign. She could keep him on edge—and keep pushing him over it—for ages. If only they had more time.

With a sinking feeling, she realized that she wanted more time with him. Of course she did. He was a gorgeous, two-dicked alien who seemed totally into her, even if he was a jerk sometimes.

But other times, he wasn't.

It had to be lust making her want more of him—more of this. Who wouldn't want more? There was no way she was falling for him already. Or at all.

She squeezed his shaft harder, enjoying the way the ridges felt beneath her fingers. With how worked up she already was, she doubted she'd need much time to climax at all, once that other dick of his was buried deep inside her. Just the thought sent more thrilling tingles shooting through her core.

Nuar groaned as she rose up higher on her knees, changing the angle so she could fit more of him in her mouth. She sped up her hand, increased the pressure of her tongue, and felt the first pulse as his hot seed hit the back of her throat.

"Lian," he bellowed, his hips bucking against her as she kept up with his movements, matching her lips, her hand, her head to the cadence of his release.

Her core was throbbing. She wished she was already naked so he could just plow into her with that other rock-hard dick of his. She wished this could go on forever.

She let his dick slide from her mouth and stared up at him, slowly starting to work on his other shaft again.

With a smirk, she said, "Now, you may touch me."

Chapter Ten

If Lian hadn't given Nuar permission to touch her, he would have exploded on the spot. He grabbed her under her arms and lifted her to her feet, smashing his mouth against hers.

Careful. Careful. I must be gentle.

And yet, after the powerful experience she'd just given him, he was having trouble holding himself back. She hadn't seemed to hold back any of herself with him.

He plunged into her mouth with his tongue, dominating her, letting her know that he would give her the same pleasure she'd given him—if without the agonizing restraint of not being allowed to touch her back. Now, he was free, and he intended to make sure she longed for his touch for the rest of their lives.

He thrust his thigh between her legs, pressing it against her core. Her heat blasted him even through the denim of her jeans.

Bringing his hands to her ass, he squeezed its softness, pulling her closer. She groaned, writhing against his thigh. She ran her hands down along his spines, sending white-hot waves of pleasure through his body.

He clasped her breast through her shirt, catching her nipple between his thumb and index finger and rolling it. His claws caught in the soft fabric.

That could cause a problem.

"Lian, I need you to be safe," he said.

"What like…" Her voice was breathy and she gasped as he nipped her neck. "Is there even a way things could be transmissible between us?"

"If I lose control, I don't want to hurt you."

"Oh. Yeah. That would be bad."

He ran his teeth gently over her skin and she whimpered. He wanted to hear more of that, to do whatever it took to have her begging for him. But he had to be safe about it.

Releasing her, he stepped back.

She looked bewildered at first, a haze of lust clouding her eyes. But then she glared at him. It seemed to be her default expression—and he found himself absolutely loving it. She was full of a fire that warmed his hearts and cleansed his soul.

Careful not to laugh, though her willingness to pursue their connection had him nearly euphoric, he kept his expression serious as he said, "It's time for you to be naked as well."

"Right," she said. "This'll be fun."

Her tone didn't match her words, though she began to

undress. In fact, she disrobed faster than he'd ever seen someone do so before. When she was done, she grabbed several blankets from the couch and tossed them on the floor in a sort of makeshift nest.

He felt his claws extend farther as he gazed on her body.

So many curves to explore. Her full hips and shapely ass, the soft round of her belly. He couldn't wait to hold the fullness of her breasts in his hands.

Instead of embracing her glory, she crossed her arms over her chest and hunched her shoulders. Again, he almost laughed, except in that moment, she seemed fragile in a way he would never have guessed possible.

"Lian," he said. "Do you not know that you are beautiful?"

She snorted and looked away. "Yeah, right. I have a potato chip habit."

He had no idea what potato chips were, but would find out as soon as possible and shower her with them.

He approached her cautiously and brushed away the curtain of dark hair that had fallen across her face. His thumb trailed along her cheekbone, then over her lush mouth.

Leaning down so his lips were almost touching hers, he said, "You are perfect in every way."

He claimed her lips again, wrapping his arms around her, feeling her skin against his. It was the most divine torture to have her so close and yet not be inside of her, not feel their souls connected through an established bond.

He could feel that bond reaching from each of them. His hearts beat strongly in synch, both with each other and with hers. The connection would be much more potent once they had shared their bodies completely.

But there were other things to be done first. Scales to be balanced.

He released her again, then lifted his arms and removed his wristbands. Holding them up before her, he said, "Please wear these."

"Your bracelets?"

"My wristbands."

She arched a wary brow at him. "Don't they control access to your technology?"

"I can get another pair back at the ship. I need you to wear these."

"Why?" she said.

"Because they can encircle you in a force field that will prevent me from hurting you accidentally. It will be just above your skin and you won't even know it's there."

"I guess that's okay. But they're way too big." She lifted her arms as if he wouldn't have noticed how delicate and tiny her wrists were.

He struck the wristbands together, then slid them over her hands and hummed the note to activate them for her. The metal coiled itself tighter, matching itself perfectly to her wrists.

"Oh, that is way cool." She looked up at him and said, "I'm keeping these, by the way."

His hearts pounded faster.

She has accepted my gift.

"Of course," he said.

She smirked, and he finally let himself laugh. His chest felt lighter, though suffused with energy. Energy he knew was waiting to establish their soul bond.

"Are you sure you wish to share your body with me in this way?" he asked.

"In case that appetizer wasn't clear enough, hell yes," she said.

"Well then, I believe it is my turn to pleasure you to the edge of sanity."

Her smirk deepened. "And how do you plan to do that?"

The wristbands were still active, waiting for his commands. He hummed a note that activated their limited antigravity function, lifting Lian's arms slightly above her head.

Her gaze turned wary.

"You can trust me," he said.

"I guess turnabout is fair play, since you weren't allowed to touch me." She nodded, and said, "My safe word is sauerkraut."

"I don't know what that means."

She laughed. "Sauerkraut is a super gross food. I don't know why anyone would do that to a poor, unsuspecting cabbage. I use it as my safe word, because that's the only time I'll ever mention it."

He kept staring at her, giving her time to realize her omission.

"Right, and a safe word is what I say when I've had enough and want you to stop what you're doing," she said.

"Can't you just say, 'stop,'" he asked.

"If you want to be boring about it."

He laughed again, then hummed another note, bringing her wrists higher. The wristbands latched onto each other with a clack, leaving Lian stretched before him.

He stepped in to kiss her, wanting to reassure her that he had only her pleasure in mind. Not being able to touch her had pushed him to a new level of ecstasy. He wanted to give her a similar experience.

He let himself explore her mouth, their tongues sparring. Lian wasn't passive about anything. He loved that about her.

Letting his lips rove farther down, he hummed the note to activate the field that would protect her from his teeth and claws. He kissed the nape of her neck and traced his teeth across her skin.

Her body shivered.

"That tingles," she said.

"I want you to feel all the pleasure I can give you, even

through the shield." He stepped back and ran his claws gently over her chest. Bright motes of light flickered in their wake. "It will only activate when needed, based on the specifications I programmed."

She arched an eyebrow. "So, you planned for something like this to happen while you were on Earth?"

"I had hopes, but you've already exceeded them by farther than I could have ever imagined."

She frowned. "Lucky you started off with me, then."

He cupped her cheek and said, "Now and always you are the only woman on Earth, on Cygnus-Prime, in the entire universe who interests me."

Chapter Eleven

Lian's eyes widened and her lips parted as if she was about to speak. But then she shook her head and said, "Just shut up and kiss me."

The command lacked her usual bite.

If she was feeling half the intense flood of emotion as Nuar, he understood the change in her demeanor. This was the beginning of the rest of their lives.

"That's not what I have planned next," he said.

"Oh?"

Her cheeks were bright red, the flush spreading down her neck and dusting the tops of her breasts. A perfect place to start.

He lifted them in his hands, kneading their softness. He brought one to his mouth and sucked her nipple hard enough to make her gasp.

"Okay, that works for me," she said.

Chuckling, he turned his attention to the other and did the same.

Lian's breath quickened as she clenched her thighs together. But he wanted to be the sole source of her pleasure. He pushed his thigh between hers, spreading her legs apart. She let out a frustrated grunt, bringing a smile to his lips.

Lips…

Remembering what she'd done to him with her mouth, he decided to truly balance the scales. He dropped to his knees before her, then lifted her legs and hooked them around the back of his neck. He raised himself up a bit, making sure she was comfortable as she was suspended above him, the wristbands' anti-gravity function working perfectly.

When he had her where he wanted her, he buried his mouth in the soft folds between her legs, uncurling his tongue to lap at her core.

"Nuar…" she gasped.

He could feel her pulling against the wristbands, her hips bucked against his face. An excellent start.

He pulled her clitoris between his lips, then swirled his tongue over it. Again, she gasped, her hips gyrating against him.

She had used her hands as well. He dragged a knuckle along her slit, gathering her wetness. When he reached her core, he slid two fingers in, deep.

"Nuar…"

Stars, how it hit him when she said his name. His primary cock ached with the need to be buried deep inside of her. The secondary had already recovered, and was waiting to fill her as well.

But first, he needed to see to this pleasure for her.

"You feel it, don't you?" he asked, looking up at her. "The pull to me. The bond."

Her lips parted as she nearly panted with need. "Of course I do."

"You want this? Want me?" He moved his fingers in and out.

Her eyes rolled shut and she arched her back. "Yes."

"All of me," he said, then swirled his tongue over her clitoris.

She let out a plaintive groan. "All of you. Everything."

"Forever," he said.

"Absolutely."

His hearts pounded in his chest. She would be his. They would belong to each other for all eternity.

Once their bond was established, there would be no denying that she was his soulmate—that other Cygnians could find their mates on Earth. The queen and king would have to recognize the alliance Kral was trying to form. Lian's homeworld and her people would be protected.

He clenched her ass and pressed her harder against him as he brought his lips to her most intimate place once more, increasing the speed of his fingers within her. She matched his movements, grinding against him, letting out little whimpers of need.

Her body froze, and then her hips bucked in a flurry of movement. He felt her pulsing around his fingers, her heels digging into his back on either side of his spines as she cried out.

He matched her pace, his spines taut, his body nearly on fire with the need to bury himself inside her and link their souls forever. Finally, she relaxed, dangling from the wristbands and his shoulders with a contented smile on her face.

But Nuar was far from contented.

He stood, lifting her legs from around his neck and bringing them to his waist instead. She roused a bit, hooking her ankles together behind his back.

He lined up his smaller, secondary dick at her core, pressing the primary to his stomach so that it would rub against her clitoris as he moved. With a swift stroke, he buried himself deep within her.

Pleasure rocketed through him, more intense than anything he'd ever felt before. And this wasn't even their bonding union.

Lian cried out again, arching her back. Her breasts pressed against his chest. He could feel her core start to throb around his cock.

Such softness... And she was so wet and tight.

"Nuar..."

There was no mistaking the pleading note to her voice.

He claimed her mouth, plundering her softness with his tongue as he thrust into her, again and again, pushing her fully into the climax and keeping her there for as long as he could. Only when she finally began to relax did he slow his pace and release her lips.

She let out a groan as she pulled against the wristbands. "I want to touch you."

He was glad her eyes were closed so that she couldn't see his grin of triumph. He placed his lips against her neck and hummed the note that would deactivate the anti-gravity field and release her, taking her slight weight easily and holding her against him.

She had made that nest of blankets, and he intended to make good use of it. He dropped to his knees, then pressed her onto her back in the pile of soft fabric.

She kept her legs tight against his waist and stretched her arms around him to trace his spines. Her touch sent shivers through his entire body.

Her core was still tight around him, the pulsing subsiding. He would have to do something about that.

Slowly, he pulled himself nearly from her, then thrust back in. She let out a soft sound and smiled, her eyes still shut.

"Wow, we really could do this forever," she said.

Nuar pressed his lips against the sensitive skin beneath her ear and whispered, "You have no idea."

She actually laughed. The sound vibrated out through her chest and into his.

Then she looked up at him and smiled.

Connected as they were, Nuar felt it thrum through his

chest, lighting his hearts. Tendrils of the energy within him were uncoiling and reaching for her. And with that smile, he felt the energy latent within her reach for him as well.

He increased his pace, holding her gaze as he thrust into her again and again. Her smile faded as pleasure took hold of her once more.

She angled her hips to meet each stroke, taking everything he had to give, demanding he give her all that he was. The friction and heat was too much for him to hold on any longer.

His cock pulsed along with her core, coaxed into his own climax as he pounded into her. His primary cock began to throb as well, begging for its turn.

The moment his secondary cock began to soften, he lined up his primary and buried himself as deep as he could within her.

Lian gasped, her eyes flashing open in surprise. But then they clenched shut, her head thrown back as she cried out again.

Nuar didn't stop, didn't slow his pace as he kept pounding into her, the pull of her core spurring him on, the strength of her grip on his back, her heels digging into him as she kept him as close as she could, the incredible tightness of her sheath making his nerves scream in ecstasy with each stroke.

His hearts were pounding. He could feel her answering

beat.

The energy held tight in his chest opened and poured into her as the climax hit him, his vision filling with light. He felt her within him, her energy merging with his.

Her core clenched around him, pulling forth his seed, meeting the pulse of his shaft as he kept on his near-frenzied movements.

She called out his name as he cried out, "Soulmate," in answer.

His vision began to clear. He slowed his thrusts, but couldn't quite keep himself from moving within her.

He wanted this connection, physical, mental, emotional —the connection of their souls—to last for eternity.

He kissed the side of her neck, still moving, wishing his secondary cock would harden faster so that he could bring them both to that edge again and push them over it. He settled for holding himself as deep within her as he could, trying to be patient.

Lian ran her hands up and down his back on either side of his spine. She let out another of those contented breaths, but then suddenly stiffened.

"Wait, a minute," she said. "What did you call me?"

Chapter Twelve

"Soulmate," Nuar said.

"Soulmate."

Lian's heart sank. Which was quite the roller coaster, since she'd been on Cloud 9 a moment before.

"Sauerkraut." She tapped on his shoulder when he didn't move. "Sauerkraut. Get off me."

Nuar slid from her body, making more mind numbing shivers course through her. She really, really needed to focus at the moment, though.

As soon as he'd made room, she rolled off the blankets and then hopped to her feet. Wow, she was going to be sore for a couple of days.

The physical soreness, she didn't mind. It was the heart soreness that she was pissed about.

Flashing lights caught her eye. She looked around to see rainbows all over the walls of the room. Some even seemed to be floating in the air.

"Are you doing this?" she asked Nuar.

"Yes."

"Well, stop it."

He laughed, then said, "I wouldn't want to even if I

could. It's beautiful, isn't it?"

He looked at her and smiled. She wanted to smile back. She also wanted to smack him.

"Of course, it's beautiful," she said. "The room is filled with freaking rainbows."

She wasn't sure if they were coming out of the spines on his back or what, but that wasn't what was important at the moment.

Nuar looked around the room in wonder. "I'd heard legends about the prismatic effect of bonding with one's soulmate, but never thought I'd experience it myself."

"No." Lian shook her head. "No, no, no. There is no way that I am in a soulmate story. This is…super-hot sex with a big blue alien. That's it."

"I don't understand."

"Neither did I!" She put her hands on top of her head and started pacing in the small room. Then she remembered she was naked. "I don't know what the hell I was thinking."

She gathered her clothes and started to dress as quickly as she could. Nuar followed suit.

"What do you mean?" he asked.

"This." She gestured between the two of them. "I never should have done this. It was impulsive and stupid and—"

"Sauerkraut!" he bellowed.

She paused, her jeans halfway up her legs. If he'd said any other word, she would have lit into him. But it was all so absurd…

"Listen, there has been some mistake," she said as she finished fastening her jeans. "I am no one's soulmate."

"This isn't a story, Lian." Nuar spoke so earnestly, she paused again, staring at him. "This is our lives. We are bonded."

Oh shit.

What had he said earlier? Something about forever? But that was supposed to be pillow talk. It was supposed to be meaningless.

A tiny part of her that she couldn't even face warmed at the idea that it wasn't.

Sadirians called their spouses bondmates. Lian looked at the wristbands Nuar had given her and her heart somehow both sank and soared at the same time.

Her chest felt like it had been supercharged with energy, ever since that amazing…fifth? Sixth climax? She'd lost count of how many he'd given her.

But that last one was different. Something had happened between them.

"Oh no." She stalked up to him, pointing at one of the wristbands. "Tell me that you did not marry me just now."

He let out a short laugh. "Of course not."

Again, she struggled to tell if she was relieved or disappointed. Since he was being so casual about it, she decided to go back to her default reaction—being pissed.

"How the hell am I supposed to know?" she said.

"For us to be married, one of us has to challenge the other to combat, the challenge must be accepted, and the challenger must win," he said.

She had to fight him for them to be married?

If he challenged her, that would be no problem. Assuming she decided to accept the challenge, apparently. He would win easily. But if he didn't challenge her, they'd never be married. There was no way she could defeat him.

Why am I even thinking about this?

She wanted to pull her hair out. She wanted to shriek and yell at him. No one had ever gotten under her skin like he did.

As if he was already there. In her head, her heart, her... soul.

"This sucks," she yelled.

"Don't worry. We'll figure out the challenge aspect later. The important thing is that we've activated our link and are bonded now."

She could feel it. The pull toward him wasn't as overpowering, but there was something else passing between them. She didn't understand it, and that scared her—and made her even angrier.

"That's not what I'm talking about!"

He made a frustrated sound and said, "Then what *are* you talking about?"

"We're supposed to have time! Time to get to know each other. To learn what each of us is like. We're supposed to be friends before we're lovers, and... Okay, granted, that's my bad, too. But I didn't think you were sticking around and I sure as hell didn't think we had some kind of magical connection that meant we're supposed to spend the rest of our lives together."

"I can't control the fact that we're connected."

"You could have explained things better. You could have given me a chance to decide before activating our link or whatever."

"How was *I* supposed to know?" He took a few steps toward her and dammit, her nether parts started to fire up again. "I've never loved anyone outside of my family and my prism. I've never shared my body with someone as we did or even felt the slightest interest in doing so. This is all new to me, too."

Lian was stunned. That was his debut?

"The soulmate bond is sacred among my people," he said. "The universe itself has decreed that we belong together."

Her anger fired right back up at the reminder that it wasn't *her* that interested him. Not really. It was the stupid soulmate bond.

"The universe, huh?" She shook her head and let out a disgusted snort. "That's great. But do you even like me?"

"Of course I do."

"There's no, 'of course,' about it," she yelled. "You don't even know me."

"And you don't even know me," he shouted back. "If that's your argument, why did you initiate mating?"

"Humans don't always make sense. And we sure as hell don't become permanent mates any time we hook up with someone."

She swore she could feel a rumbling vibration ripple out from him like a subsonic growl. It made all the hairs on her arms stand on end.

"Humans may not make sense, but soulmate bonds do," Nuar said. "The force that connects us is stronger than you can imagine. Eventually, you'll realize that we're perfect for each other."

She held up a hand and started counting things off on her fingers. "You destroyed my greenhouse. You shattered the bench I made with my dad. You're smug and reckless."

He mirrored her gesture, countering each point. "I'm helping to restore the plant life to what it was. I've created a replacement bench and will apologize to your father in any manner you desire. And I'm tempering all of my actions, as well as teaching my fellow warriors to temper theirs so that we can fit in with your people without causing further harm."

"Because we're soulmates," she said. "Not because you want to. Not because you care about me for *me*."

He opened his mouth, but then closed it again. Apparently, he didn't have a comeback for the truth.

Her vision blurred. Goddammit, she would not cry in front of him. Not because of this. Not because the little glimmer of hope she'd started to feel about him caring for her had been extinguished. Not because it meant way more to her than she ever imagined.

The only reason he was with her was because they were soulmates. And that wasn't enough for Lian.

"I need to go," she said.

"Lian, we just need time. You'll see that the universe is right about us belonging together."

"What I need is to be alone to process this."

"What can I do?" He looked stricken.

Her heart gave a little tug, but she ignored it.

"Don't follow me," she said. "Watch my dog."

She stormed out of her office, not waiting for a response.

He wasn't following her. She didn't have to look and check. She could *feel* it. The farther she walked away from him, the stronger the pull became to turn back.

Incensed, she picked up speed, heading away from him instead. Away from everyone.

She ended up at Horizon Park. School was in session, so the place was empty. She sat on a swing and held onto one of the chains, staring at the ground.

Pats of water hit the dirt beneath her feet. She sniffed and wiped at her cheeks.

Thank god she'd left before this happened. The last

thing she needed was Nuar knowing how much he already meant to her.

If he were with her, he'd comfort her. Wrap his strong arms around her. Pull her against his chest. And she'd feel safe and protected and...loved.

But not because of who she was. Because of some stupid soulmate bond.

How could they build a future on that?

"Lian?"

She yelped and jumped up, spinning around. Craig was perched on top of the swing set. Ellie was clinging to his stomach with her arms and legs, but was reaching toward Lian with her blue-and-white striped tentacles and making little fussing sounds.

Craig swung upside down, holding the bar with his feet and one arm and keeping another hand on Ellie.

"What's wrong?" Craig asked.

"Nothing." Lian sniffed again and quickly wiped at her eyes. "Everything's fine."

Craig let out a soft snort. He released the swing set and spun around, landing on his feet. Then he stood straight— something he didn't often do—and shook his head. Wow, he was huge.

"You are not fine," he said.

Lian felt her lip quiver. She hated that Nuar had made her feel this way. Vulnerable and weak. She'd never let anyone get to her like this before.

"Come on." Craig held open most of his arms. Ellie did the same. "You need a hug."

"No, I don't," Lian lied.

"It is a well known fact that Lyrians give the best hugs in the entire universe, though few have been lucky enough to be given one." He wiggled his fingers. "Go ahead. You know you want to."

Damn. He did look soft. And he had a lot of arms.

Lian stepped forward and Craig wrapped three of his arms around her. Ellie wrapped her tentacles around Lian's waist and twisted so she could hug Lian as well.

Okay, that was a good hug. Craig's fur was so soft and somehow not overwarm for the summer morning. Lian could barely see past all the white fluff surrounding her.

But it wasn't the best hug. Nuar's were the best hugs.

Craig sat back on the ground, pulling Lian with him and perching her on his leg. He kept two arms on her back.

It was like being snuggled by a giant bear. Only with more arms. And less biting her face off.

"Tell me," he said.

"I hate Nuar."

Craig's eyebrows lifted. "Really? Why?"

"He… He wrecked the greenhouse."

"I was there, too," Craig said. "Do you hate me?"

"Of course not."

"It would make more sense for you to blame me, though. I've been visiting Earth for a very long time. I know more about your ways and I've lived in Harbor for months. I should have known better."

"Yeah, you should have," she said, glowering.

"Then why aren't you mad at me?"

"Well, I am mad at you."

"No, you aren't."

He was right. Lian scrambled to explain why. "You helped build the greenhouse in the first place. You helped transform Harbor into what it is now."

"A town meant for aliens to visit and get to know more about Earthlings, as well as each other. A place where we can learn how to get along."

"Yeah."

"You don't expect every alien who visits to already know the rules and follow them, do you?"

"Of course not."

"Then why are you being so hard on Nuar? He's never been to Earth before. In fact, most Cygnians never leave their system. It's unusual that they're venturing out now and that's something we should encourage."

"So, I should just give him a pass for every misstep he makes?"

Craig laughed. "Then he wouldn't learn anything. I'm just pointing out that this kind of thing is what Harbor is for."

She highly doubted that.

"There's…something else." Her face heated.

Craig tilted his head, waiting.

"Apparently, Nuar and I are *soulmates*." She shoved as much contempt as she could into the word.

"You're kidding," Craig said. "Are you sure?"

"If the rainbow aftereffects are to be believed."

"After..." Craig's eyebrow ridge lifted. "Oh, that's what that scent is."

"Excuse me?"

"I've never encountered the Cygnian mating scent."

"Ew." Lian shoved against Craig's chest, to no effect.

"This is interesting," Craig said. "I thought Cygnians could only have that connection with other Cygnians."

"Lucky me, I'm the exception."

"You aren't happy about it?"

"I might have been, if things had happened differently. But I didn't have time to think about what was going on or to get to know him or anything."

Craig laughed again. "Lian, you are among my favorite people. You're one of the very few sentients outside our family that we entrust with Ellie. I think I know you fairly well."

"And?"

"And if you'd had enough time to think about establishing a bond with Nuar, even after having time to get to know him, you would have thought yourself right out of it."

"Hey!"

"Am I wrong?"

She grumbled, turning her attention to Ellie. Lian held one set of the little Lyrian's hands and bounced them gently up and down while she tried to ignore Craig's question.

The trouble was, Craig was right.

Lian hated how vulnerable she felt right now. And she knew it would only get worse the more she cared for Nuar.

If they'd had a chance to date, she would have cared even more, and that would have scared the crap out of her. She would have run away.

Just like she was doing now.

"Are those his wristbands that you're wearing?" Craig asked.

"Yeah. I forgot to ask him to take them back."

"You don't want to keep them? It's a significant gesture. There are many factions who would love to get their hands on Cygnian technology."

"Great."

Craig was silent for a few moments, then said, "In all my centuries, I have observed that things happen for a reason, even if we don't appreciate the timing at first. The universe has a way of making things fall into place when and where they need to."

Lian continued to grumble.

"Do you feel connected to him?" Craig asked.

"Well, yeah. Especially after…" Her cheeks prickled.

"But even before, I bet you did."

Again, she couldn't deny it.

"Barbara and I can smell when an Earthling and a Sadirian are a match for pair-bonding," Craig said.

"Eww, gross." Lian bumped his chest with her shoulder.

"It's just the pheromones their bodies put off. We can tell when there's good biochemistry. But Cygnian soulmates." He shook his head. "That kind of connection is on an entirely different level. Cygnians are all about light. Frequencies and wavelengths beyond most normal physical existence. I can see where it might be frightening to experience."

"That's not it," Lian said, her voice small. "I hate the thought that he's only interested in me because we're soulmates."

"Then ignore it. It's just a thought." Craig gave her a squeeze. "Do you know why we like you?"

"No."

"Because you always give us crap," he said.

"Wow, that's great. My sarcasm and glare endear me to many life forms."

"They do."

She'd been joking. She sighed as Ellie settled in her lap, looking up at Lian with those adorable blue eyes.

"You never once were overly nice to us just because we're aliens or because you're intimidated by our magnificence." Craig grinned when Lian chuckled. "That's kind of amazing—and it's just who you are. Don't you think he sees that, too?"

"Maybe," she said.

"I think you both elicit such strong emotions from each other because of the soulmate bond. You don't understand it, so you call it 'hate' to reassure yourself. But I don't think that's how you really feel about him."

"Fine," Lian said. "Be right."

Craig laughed again. "And speaking of strong reactions elicited by mates, Barbara is going to rip off my arms if I don't meet her back at the ship. We're supposed to talk to Doc about repairing one of the cars I landed on while Nuar and I were fighting."

Lian stood along with him. "Thanks for the talk."

"Any time, little nestling." He reached over and ruffled her hair.

"I'm not a nestling. Quit it." She shoved his hand away and smoothed down the mess he'd probably made.

"In case you hadn't noticed, you're all nestlings to me." He winked, then reached for Ellie.

The *actual* nestling started to cry, clinging tightly to Lian.

"Oh, come on, sweetling," Craig said. "Barbara really will be angry if I don't meet her soon."

"I can watch her," Lian said.

"Are you sure?"

"Yeah. We'll play here a bit and then I'll take her back to the library. You can pick her up there when you're done."

"Lian, you are a treasure." Craig gave her a quick hug, then leaned down and brushed the side of his head against Ellie's. "You behave."

Ellie ignored him, grabbing a lock of Lian's hair and starting to chew on it.

Craig took a few steps away, waved, then dropped to all...sixes...and stampeded off. It was really the only way to describe it.

Lian pulled her hair from Ellie's mouth, then reached into her purse and pulled out a squeaky toy. Ever since she'd caught Ellie in Ed's toy box, Lian had made sure to always have some fresh, clean dog toys on hand.

Ellie squealed in delight, then grabbed the toy and started squeezing it over and over. Lian sat back down on the swing, gently rocking them back and forth. Her mind was spinning, going over everything Craig had said.

He was right. Given a chance, Lian would absolutely have talked herself out of any kind of commitment to Nuar.

He was an alien. Her parents wouldn't approve. Oh God, how was she going to tell her parents about this?

They couldn't have kids, apparently.

She wanted to have kids. She'd always imagined herself having them. But when she pictured it now, Nuar was right there with her, laughing as their kids did something silly. Or it was him lifting the child into the air, a huge smile on his face.

Am I really thinking about this?

She was. She absolutely was.

And the more she let herself think about it, the more she loved the idea. She remembered his expression when he'd thought he might get to see a child in the library and her heart gave a little lurch. He obviously wanted kids, too. Maybe they could adopt.

Nuar had been an oblivious asshat when they first met. But as soon as he'd realized what he was doing, he'd stopped. Maybe he'd needed the incentive of her being his soulmate, but once he figured that out, he'd turned it around and tried to fix his mistakes.

She had a feeling he would do anything for her. No one outside of her family and best friends had ever made Lian feel that way. Certainly not the few guys she'd tried dating in college.

Nuar would cherish her. He would cherish their kids and Lian's family. She had no doubt of it.

Sure, it freaked her out a little that he had so much faith in the universe that he would throw in everything with Lian so quickly. But what if the universe was right? What if Nuar was Lian's perfect mate and she was about to miss out on everything he had to offer?

Love and support. Adventure and passion. Could she

really walk away from that? Thinking about it made her chest ache.

The other path—the amazing potential of what their lives could be like together—was exhilarating. The more she thought about that path, the more excited she became. She had a soulmate. A single person in the universe who was meant for her and who she was meant to be with.

Her soulmate was a seven foot tall, gorgeous, blue alien. A Cygnian warrior.

Her Cygnian warrior.

And she'd left him at the library.

She stood up, hugging Ellie tight to her chest. Ellie started to cry.

"Sweetie, I'm sorry I need to cut our park time short," Lian said. "But I promise I'll make it up to you next time. We have to—"

The last word froze in Lian's throat. She couldn't speak or move, except for her eyes. Looking around frantically at what she could see in front of her, she tried to figure out what was going on.

A large metal box floated into her field of vision. She'd used similar ones in the greenhouse to haul around heavy plants. An anti-gravity platform.

This one had sides and a lid. It was big enough to fit a person into.

Her heart was pounding. Ellie had stopped crying—or at least, Lian couldn't hear it anymore. Whatever was affecting Lian, it was affecting the little Lyrian as well. She could still feel Ellie at least, the flutter of her hearts and the tight grip of her hands and feet.

Someone pushed the box further into Lian's field of view.

Gary?

"Hello, Lian," Gary said.

He was pointing a small silver disk at her. She'd seen one before in an educational video when Harbor was first learning about their new alien neighbors. A stasis disk.

"I'd say I'm sorry about this, but it's actually great to get you along with the nestling," he said. "She likes you."

He tipped the anti-gravity box up so that it was running alongside Lian's body, then maneuvered it next to her. With his other hand, he lifted the stasis disk.

Lian felt like gravity had gone all kinds of crazy. Up was sideways and down was diagonal.

She could see the ground moving in relation to her body, letting her know she was floating. Then she was drifting into the box and couldn't see anything.

Anything except Gary.

He stepped in front of her, slipping the disk into his pocket. His gaze dropped to Ellie and he smiled.

"A Lyrian," he said. "This is incredible." He looked up at Lian. "Thank you so much for your help."

She was going to help him to her foot up his ass the moment she could move again.

"I would never have been able to get Ellie away from Craig or Barbara. I knew it would be much simpler to obtain her from an Earthling."

Earthlings... Wait, wasn't Gary an Earthling?

For a moment, her mind froze with terror. Was this another identity of Dean, the Scorpiian shapeshifter that had some weird interest in Harbor?

The Vegans said they were scanning for him, though. They would have detected him.

No, Gary was something else. Something they couldn't detect—or who didn't set off any warnings.

"The High Council has been trying to get Lyrian DNA for thousands of years," he said. "I never thought I'd be the one to finally manage it."

Was he one of the misguided Sadirians who missed the High Council? But why was he talking about them as if they were still around?

"This is a step toward peace and safety," Gary said. "You'll understand eventually. But it's very important that you cooperate once we get to my ship."

Her heart sank. Panic set in as he smiled, then closed the lid to the box, plunging them into darkness.

She had to do something. She had to help Ellie escape.

If Nuar were here, he would pound Gary into the ground. Hell, even Ed would—

Her heart sank further as she realized the clue she'd missed. Ed had bitten Gary. Ed, the super sweet dog who could barely be bothered to get up for a snack and never growled at anyone, had *bitten* Gary.

This wasn't the first time he'd tried to take Ellie.

Lian should have seen it. She should have done something to prevent this. Even her dog had done a better job protecting Ellie.

She had no idea where Gary was going to take them after they reached his ship—or what he had planned beyond... Beyond extracting DNA from Ellie.

Lian's eyes blurred with tears at the thought.

None of this would have happened if she'd stayed with Nuar. If she hadn't freaked out about her feelings for him. About their soulmate connection.

Connection...

Craig had said Cygnian bonds were about frequencies and wavelengths. Lian didn't really understand any of it. But if the universe was going to throw its weight around and say she and Nuar were soulmates, Lian was going to use that to try to get her and Ellie some help.

She turned her thoughts inward and focused with all her might on Nuar—on willing him to know where she was and that she was in trouble. That she needed him and...that she wanted him. More than anything.

She closed her eyes and prayed it would be enough.

Chapter Thirteen

Watching Lian leave went against every instinct in Nuar's body. He wanted to charge after her, throw her over his shoulder, and take her to his quarters on the ship.

He would need to prepare his quarters, though. Even the floor of her office was too hard for her. The blankets she'd thrown down were evidence of that.

He picked one up, examining the fabric.

Soft and flimsy. Bron could craft better, but he would need this as an example of what Earthlings used for their comfort.

Nuar looked around Lian's office for more clues as to what would make her happy with him. The couch had cushions all over it. That was important. He lifted one from the seat and tucked it under his arm, then draped the blanket over his shoulder.

"Hello, I'm back," Olivia called from the other room. "Guys? The library was supposed to open fifteen minutes ago. I gave you a little extra time to…work things out."

Nuar stepped into the main room. Olivia was visible down a row of shelves.

"Oh, hello there." She smiled at him and looked

around. "Where's Lian?"

"She said she had to leave," Nuar said.

"She left you here alone? That's not right."

"She needed time to process things." Alone. Without her soulmate.

That was not right.

He wanted Lian to be able to turn to him. He needed to support her. But he was realizing he had no idea how to do so.

"May I speak with you?" Nuar asked.

"Isn't that what we're doing?"

"Forgive me. I meant may I speak with you candidly."

"I prefer it."

Nuar smiled. Here was a woman, like Lian, who spoke her mind and expected others to do the same.

"Cygnian women are warriors," he said.

"Like you."

He laughed. "They are much fiercer."

"Really?" Olivia said. "I think I like the sound of your planet."

He smiled at the compliment.

"They are…decisive," he said.

"Okay."

"Lian is…"

Olivia nodded. "Lian is not. In fact, if you hang out with more Earthlings, I bet you'll find a lot of us can change our mind quite a bit."

"How do you function? How do you move forward if you need to analyze and rethink every decision?"

"Well, we don't analyze everything. Sometimes, the more important something is, the more time we need to think about it. I consider it more a strength than a weakness."

"How so?"

"If we realize we're wrong, we can change."

He nodded. "True. We Cygnians are slow to change. And when we believe we know something, we simply plow forward with single-minded purpose."

"Kind of how you and Craig plowed through the greenhouse?"

"I suppose so."

"Did you know my brother is the mayor?" she asked.

"I didn't."

"He goes on and on about how Harbor is a place where aliens can learn about Earthlings and how everyone can get along if we work at it. The whole point of this town is for us to be able to change and adapt and coexist. All of us, not just our visitors. We Earthlings have things to learn from you, too."

"Why do I feel like there's a point you're trying to make that eludes me?"

Olivia laughed. "Lian overthinks everything. She's brilliant, creative, and passionate."

His chest swelled with pride at each word. Of course,

his soulmate was amazing. He hadn't doubted it and looked forward to discovering more about her throughout their lives together. He knew the universe would bring him to someone he could respect and appreciate. She was the other half of his soul, after all.

"But she can also get stuck in her own head," Olivia continued. "Seeing how she is with you... I don't know. I guess I have a feeling maybe you can snap her out of that. Get her moving forward finally."

"Really?"

"Yeah. I've never seen her so worked up over a guy before. Over anyone, actually. I'm curious to see where it goes."

"As am I."

"Well, don't worry about her needing some time. She'll come around."

Nuar nodded. "Could you fasten the lead to Ed? I need to return to my ship so I can prepare my quarters for Lian."

Olivia's eyes widened. "Whoa, I said she needed time. Don't you think that's moving a little fast?"

"Things...have already progressed."

"Progressed how?" Olivia crossed her arms and stared at him in a similar—if much less intense—fashion as Lian.

"We are soulmates," Nuar said.

"Soulmates?" Her eyes widened. "For real?"

"Yes. But she wasn't happy about us bonding."

Olivia dropped her arms and took a few steps closer. "Wait, you guys are married?"

"Of course not. She thought the same thing. Why do you all think that?"

"Because that's what Sadirians call getting married."

Nuar barely managed not to sneer. If he was going to win Lian over, he needed her friends on his side, and her friends included Sadirians. He needed to make peace with the fact that he would be living alongside the Coalition for as long as he and Lian were together—which he hoped would be a very long time.

"Cygnian marriages are different," Nuar said. "Lian and I have established our soul bond."

"And how did you do that?"

"We mated."

Olivia's mouth dropped open. "In the *library*?"

"No, of course not in the library. In her office."

"That's barely better."

"Lian was upset that she didn't understand the implications of our union."

"So, she left." Olivia nodded. "That's rough. But I still have hope for you guys. Just give her time to come around."

He nodded. "I still need to prepare my quarters. For when she's ready."

"You can leave Ed with me."

"Lian asked me to watch over him."

Olivia smiled. "That's a very good sign. If she trusts you with her dog, she definitely has feelings for you."

"Yes, antipathy. Anger."

He could practically feel them rolling off of Lian after their mating. And yet, there had been undercurrents of something else. Hope and...fear. Somehow, the fear seemed to be rising in her. He could still feel it, even with the distance between them.

"Lian is always angry," Olivia said. "It's part of her charm. But she's also the most loyal friend you'll ever have."

"Do you know why she would have any reason to be afraid of a union with me?"

"Lian hasn't had much luck with guys over the years. She busts stereotypes all over the place. She hasn't met the man who can handle how unique and awesome she is." Olivia smiled. "Well, she *hadn't*, anyway."

"Those men were fools," Nuar said.

Olivia's smile deepened. She nodded, then headed to a counter and retrieved Ed's lead. The dog rose when he saw it and stood still while she attached it to his collar.

As Olivia handed the lead to Nuar, she said, "Lian is like a sister to me. Don't hurt her, okay?"

"I will do everything in my power to keep her happy and safe."

A twinge shot down his spine. Was she safe now?

She had to be. This was Harbor, a town protected by

Vegans. They wouldn't let anything happen to their allies.

But it should be *Nuar* who was protecting her.

"Good," Olivia said.

His agitation growing, Nuar turned and made his way from the library, Ed at his side. The day was growing warmer and the sun shone brightly overhead.

Where had Lian gone? Was she thinking of him? Was she still angry?

As he thought of her, he could feel her on the edge of his mind. He had a sense that she had gone in a different direction than where he was heading. He wanted to turn around and go to her, but she had told him not to follow. Still, the urge to run to her was strong.

He needed to get to his ship. Immediately. His prism could help him sort this out.

Ed looked up at him and whined. The dog was drooling more than usual.

That thick coat wouldn't help him in this heat. The hangar was still a mile away, and there weren't many trees between the spaceport and the town.

"Come here, friend," Nuar said, kneeling down.

Ed walked over to him and waited patiently. Nuar shifted the blanket around his neck, then lifted the dog onto his shoulders so that he rested on top of it. He picked up the cushion as he stood.

His wristbands would have been welcome at that moment. He could have used their antigravity function to carry the gear, or made an environmental control field around Ed to cool the animal. As soon as Nuar reached the *Arrow*, he would get another pair.

At least he knew that Lian had that much protection. When they were together, Nuar would be able to activate and control her wristbands. It would be that much easier to keep her safe.

With Ed on his shoulders, Nuar wasn't limited by the dog's pace. He picked up his speed, quickly covering the distance between him and the ship. A sense of urgency was growing within him that he didn't understand.

When he reached the hangar, he realized he didn't have a way to communicate with the warriors on board the ship. He was about to set Ed down and find something to throw at the ship to get their attention when the bottom hatch opened. Kral, Lar, and Dorn stood inside, just at the edge of the opening, their expressions clouded with worry.

"Hang on, friend," Nuar said. Ed let out a little whine.

Nuar leapt up into the ship. The dog started struggling against Nuar's shoulders the moment they landed. Nuar held onto him as Dorn closed the hatch. He had promised Lian he would keep Ed safe. That was a promise he meant to keep.

But what of Lian herself?

Nuar had a terrible feeling that something was wrong. He just didn't know what to do about it.

"What's going on?" Lar asked, worry narrowing his

golden eyes. "We sensed your distress."

Kral gestured at Nuar's bare wrists. "Where are your wristbands?"

Dorn stepped in front of them, holding his hand up to motion them back. He stared at Nuar, and said, "What is that thing on your neck?"

"This is Ed," Nuar said. "He's Lian's dog."

Kral laughed. "That's not a dog."

"It is." Nuar shoved past them. "We don't have time for this."

As soon as they reached the common room, he dropped to his knees and leaned forward, setting Ed gently on the ground. The dog turned to him and woofed, then trotted toward one of the benches, his nose tracing scents along the floor.

"Something is wrong." Nuar dropped the cushion and blanket he'd been carrying on the floor in a pile. Ed came over and settled down on them, flopping over to sleep.

"If you've lost your wristbands, I'd say so," Kral said.

Dorn shrugged. "Only a Cygnian would know how to use them."

The rest of the prism was already in the room. Rom and Bron stood across from them and even Tarn had come up from the engine room.

"I didn't lose my wristbands," Nuar said. "I gave them to Lian."

"That's great," Rom said, a smile lighting his face.

"She accepted you."

"Not...exactly." Nuar shook his head. "We've bonded, but there was a problem."

"I told you we wouldn't find our soulmates on Earth," Lar said.

"No, the connection is there," Nuar insisted. "I can feel it. But Lian didn't understand that mating would activate our soulmate bond. She didn't react well when she found out."

"Why not?" Kral asked.

"She isn't sure she wants the link." Nuar's hearts felt heavy as he spoke the words.

"If it's a true soulmate bond, it will be there whether she wants it or not," Tarn said.

Kral shook his head. "This could complicate our future relations with Earth."

"I'm not concerned about that." Nuar started pacing the room, his claws extending. He wanted to throw something.

"Then what is agitating you?" Kral asked.

"I don't know." Nuar ran his hands through his hair. "I feel as though I'm crawling out of my skin and that there's nothing I can do about it."

"Lian will come around," Rom said. "I can give you some tips to help win her over."

"Rom has proven popular with the locals already." Tarn grinned.

"It's not that." Nuar didn't know how to describe the

emotion rising within him. He'd never felt anything like it before. He pressed both hands to the sides of his chest over his hearts, feeling their strong, unified beat.

His hearts were beating fast, but they were still synchronized. Did that mean they were following Lian's heartbeat? But if so, why was her heart racing?

"I think...I'm terrified," Nuar said.

The warriors exchanged glances, each of them standing straighter. They had entered battle together time and again, and yet Nuar had never felt more afraid.

Kral approached and rested both hands on Nuar's shoulders.

"You will not lose her," Kral said. "I promise you that."

"But I'm going to," Nuar said. "I think I already have."

"Nuar—" Kral began.

Nuar shoved him away, hard enough that Kral flew across the room and hit the wall. He bounced off and landed in a crouch, ready to receive an attack.

But he wasn't the one who Nuar needed to fight. There was someone else. Nuar wasn't sure who or even where they were.

"I need wristbands," Nuar said. "Quickly."

Kral rose and nodded to Dorn. Dorn pressed a control on the wall, opening a storage locker. He pulled out a set of wristbands and tossed them to Nuar.

As soon as Nuar plucked them from the air, he slid

them on and activated them, striking them together and humming a note to bring up the ship's computer interface. An image of Harbor appeared before them—a perfect, scaled-down replica of the town and surrounding area.

Nuar rotated his hands, changing the angle of the hologram and zooming in on a large wooded area. Strange constructs were spread throughout the space, most of it a mix of metal and brightly-colored plastics.

"What is that place?" Tarn asked.

"It's a playground," Lar said. "Vay took us there during the tour you skipped."

Tarn shrugged. "I don't like being away from the ship."

Why would Lian have gone there? Nuar was certain that she had. He scanned the area, but there weren't any Earthlings in the vicinity.

He closed his eyes and took a deep breath, letting his awareness expand. He opened his eyes and pointed.

"There," he said. "Lian is there."

Lar stepped forward and took control of the hologram, enlarging the building Nuar had pointed toward. It was a small living domicile on the edge of town near the playground.

"This is a private quarters," Lar said. "A house. Lian is probably visiting a friend."

Nuar shook his head sharply. "No, she's afraid. I can feel it. She's there. Wait…"

He pointed toward the house, and then his arm rose. He

reached out as if he could pluck her out of the air, but nothing was there. Not even in the hologram.

Lar activated their scanners, imposing grid lines and sensor readings over the images. "There's nothing."

"I'm telling you, I feel her moving," Nuar said. "And she's terrified."

"Rom," Kral said.

Rom nodded, then ran down the corridor toward the pilot's chamber. Kral turned to Bron, who slammed a fist against the wall.

Light cascaded out from the impact, activating the room's full combat array. Dorn took up his position next to the weapons station. Tarn was already gone, no doubt heading to engineering.

The hologram zoomed out, showing the entire town again, complete with their ship flying out of its hangar. The subterranean defense grid lit up, along with the power supply lines and water pipes.

"Do you think the Vegans know we can see this much of their infrastructure?" Lar asked.

"I don't care," Kral said. "Show me everything."

Lar nodded, furthering the scan.

Life forms were illuminated everywhere—green for Vegans, yellow for Earthlings, bright blue for Lyrians, and orange for Antareans.

"Which of these are Sadirians?" Lar asked.

"Yellow," Bron said. "Their bioscans are so similar to

Earthlings, we can't differentiate between them."

"I don't like that at all," Kral said.

"I'm working on it," Bron said.

"She's leaving the planetary atmosphere." Nuar's eyes were fixed on what appeared as nothing more than empty space, yet he was certain Lian was there. He just couldn't tell the exact location.

"And so are we," Bron said.

The images of Harbor fell behind as a star field and planets filled the holodisplay instead. Nuar kept pointing, following where he sensed Lian's movements.

"Anything more you can give me?" Rom's voice sounded over the comm. "I have my navigation feeds hooked into your interaction with the scans, but I'd like to get out in front of this."

"I'm doing what I can," Nuar said.

Lar angled his head. "Kral, we're being hailed by the *Reckoning*."

"Ignore it." Kral's focus was intent on the holodisplay.

Lar persisted. "They're asking if we need assistance."

"Cygnians do not require assistance," Bron said.

Nuar felt his hearts beating, his breath catching in his chest. If it meant saving Lian, he would do anything.

"Kral," Nuar said, a pleading tone to his voice unlike anything he'd ever uttered.

Kral met his gaze through the transparent display between them, then shook his head. "Until we know more, we do this on our own."

Chapter Fourteen

Light flooded Lian's vision, making her wince. She wrapped her arms around Ellie protectively, holding the nestling tight against her chest as gravity reasserted itself.

Lian's feet touched down in the bottom of the giant box she was in. She leaned against the side of it, trying to regain her balance and figure out where she was and how she could make a run for it.

There was a thin layer of light rippling over the front of the box. It made a faint buzzing sound. She had a feeling she wasn't quite as free to escape as she might think.

"Hello." Gary stepped in front of the opening of her tiny prison. He was wearing a silver catsuit with a broad belt and bracers that covered both of his forearms—the same uniforms she'd seen members of the Coalition wear.

Lian would have punched him, but she didn't want to let go of Ellie. Instead, she angled herself so that Ellie was half-obscured by Lian's body.

Gary smiled. "I appreciate your protective instincts toward the Lyrian. And she seems to have bonded with you well. If you can keep her happy—" He paused, his smile dimming. "Well, it will go better for you if you can."

"Go to hell," Lian said.

Gary laughed. "Earthlings have such interesting concepts about what happens after the body breaks down."

"Unlike you Sadirians."

She glared at him, willing him to confirm her suspicions. At least then she would know what she was dealing with.

All she knew for sure was that she was terrified—and that she wished Nuar was with her more than anything. He would wipe the floor with this guy, then safely whisk Lian and Ellie back to Earth.

"We know exactly what comes next," Gary said. "We control it. I was even part of the project that developed the transfer procedure. A minor assistant, but still."

What the hell was he talking about?

His gaze slid down to Ellie. "To think that I will be responsible for providing Lyrian DNA to the High Council."

"The High Council was destroyed," Lian said.

Gary's smile deepened. So did the dread in the pit of Lian's stomach.

"Please come with me." Gary stepped back from the box and tapped on the controls of one of his bracers.

Compared to the sleek Cygnian wristbands that seemed to be made of nothing but smooth metal, his were a cumbersome mess of buttons, panels, and lights. Still, the buzzing field in front of her vanished.

"I'm sure you're thinking of trying to escape," he said. "You should know that my bracers are equipped with the same technology as the stasis disk, as well as full offensive capabilities. I think Ellie would be upset if I had to stun you."

Lian kept glaring at him as she stepped out of her box and into a small room. The featureless walls were smooth gray metal, as were the ceiling and floor. Gary was keeping a healthy distance. He gestured toward an open doorway that led to a hall.

As they walked past him, Ellie growled. Lian patted her back and shushed her, not wanting to antagonize their captor.

The corridor was a darker gray metal, with a single red stripe at about waist level running along the walls. Three other doorways were not far down the hall. Two were on either side of their path and one was straight ahead.

The one ahead was open. Lian could see a dark window at the far end of a somewhat larger room. Was it night already? How long had she been in the box?

Her steps slowed as she realized it wasn't a nighttime sky she was seeing. It was space.

Gary had taken them off the planet. They were in a spaceship heading for who knew where.

Lian had daydreamed about leaving Earth, but she'd always thought she'd be working with a terraforming team on Mars or helping to restore damaged ecosystems like the ones on the Antarean homeworld. She'd thought it would be a trip full of excitement and hope.

This was terrifying.

She tried to clamp down her fear, not wanting Ellie to pick up on it. The little Lyrian was clinging to Lian's chest with a tight grip, staring at Gary with wide blue eyes and still letting out a low growl.

He paused at the door to their right and said, "I really must thank you for your help. There are so few people Craig and Barbara let watch their nestling. You were my best chance at securing her. When Ed wasn't around, anyway."

"If you want to thank me, take me back to Earth," Lian said.

"My supervisor wouldn't like that."

Was it Lian's imagination, or had Gary blanched a little? It passed quickly. He pressed a panel next to the door and it opened.

Lian peered inside cautiously. The room was small, with a bunk and something that looked like a sink and toilet in a corner.

"It's not much, but with a ship this small, efficiency takes priority," Gary said. "I think you should be able to figure out all the facilities. You won't be on board long."

"Where are you taking us?"

"Please." He gestured for her to enter the room.

She didn't want to be paralyzed again—or stunned.

Holding her head high, she stepped inside.

Gary lingered in the doorway. "I'm taking you to a facility with a full genetics laboratory. They'll be so excited to have access to a Lyrian nestling. No one's ever been able to obtain one before."

"You mean *kidnap*."

"Semantics." He shrugged. "I like you, Lian. I hope we can work together on this project. It will make things more...pleasant for you."

Her skin started to crawl. He wasn't looking at her lasciviously, but still, it was ultra-creepy.

"I already have a boyfriend," she quipped.

He angled his head, as if he didn't believe her. "Wait, the Cygnian?"

Should she play up her relationship with Nuar? Maybe Gary would think twice about taking a Cygnian warrior's soulmate. Or would it make things worse for her and Ellie?

Lian wasn't sure what to say, so she defaulted to her usual—she glared at him.

"This is wonderful," Gary said. "You're even more useful than I thought."

Great.

Gary took a step closer, joining her in the room. Lian lurched back, again angling away so that she was between him and Ellie again.

He didn't seem to be focusing on Ellie, though. This

time, he was focused on Lian, which was good.

It was her fault Ellie was in this situation. Craig had trusted Lian, and she had let him down.

She bit the inside of her cheek, pushing back against the burning in her eyes. No way in hell would she cry in front of this creep.

"I thought those looked like Cygnian wristbands, but had no idea how you would have secured them," Gary said. "I should be able to assist you with staying alive longer with this knowledge."

They're planning to kill me?

Her cheeks started to tingle and the room spun a bit. It felt as though all the blood had dropped out of her head and was pooling in her stomach.

She had to keep it together. Ellie was counting on her.

"You better keep me alive," Lian said. "Or Nuar will rip you apart when he finds you."

Gary shook his head, smiling again. "He'll never find me. This ship is outfitted with a Centauran cloak."

Centaurans? They were part of the Tau Centauran Assembly that had declared war with the Coalition of Planets and destroyed their High Council.

The only downside of the High Council being gone was that the Assembly had taken out the entire Sadirian home system in their attack. They'd destroyed every colony and space station in the system, as well as blowing up Sadr-4, their homeworld.

Now, they seemed to be determined to wipe out every single Sadirian settlement in the universe. The refugees had been coming to the Sol system, rallying around Earth.

Why would Centaurans be working with a Sadirian? And why would a Sadirian work with them?

She would have found it easier to believe he was that Scorpiian shapeshifter. Scorpiians were supposedly mercenaries and assassins.

Maybe she was wrong about Gary. From what Lian knew, most of the sentients who had become part of the Coalition of Planets when the High Council was in charge had genetically engineered themselves to look Sadirian— which meant most of them looked like Earthlings as well.

Gary could just be wearing a Coalition uniform. He could be Centauran or— She shivered at the thought that he might be a Tau Ceti. She would almost *rather* he be a Scorpiian.

Aside from the High Council, the Tau Ceti were the worst aliens she'd heard of. They started off their lives by cannibalizing the rest of their brood and had been feeding off of human blood like vampires.

There were too many possibilities. None of them were good.

"Not even the Vegans can see through this vessel's cloak," Gary said.

"I'm not buying it." Lian had the impression that the Vegans could do just about anything with their technology.

"The Vegans are not as all-powerful as they'd like others to believe. If you want to survive, you should remember that."

"So, you're a Centauran," Lian said.

He laughed. "No, I'm Sadirian."

"But you said this ship has Centauran technology..."

"Yes. They're working with the Tau Ceti to help restore order to the galaxy. The Assembly shares technology between their people. The Centaurans would never work with a Sadirian, but the Tau Ceti assigned to monitor the Sol system are much more open-minded."

Lian actually gasped. "How can you work with them?"

"We all have goals," Gary said. "Our alliances form around them. The Assembly is simply a means to an end."

"And what end is that?"

He actually looked a bit sad. "One you won't live to see, I'm afraid. But I can make what remains of your time more palatable if you cooperate."

"You know I won't."

He nodded. "If you only had yourself to consider, I have no doubt of that. But with Ellie in the picture, I think we can come to an understanding. The Tau Ceti scientists are not as sympathetic in their treatment of test subjects as I am."

Her blood chilled.

"Alliances and goals, Lian," Gary said. "Think hard

about what you want your last few weeks or months to be like. I think you'll decide that working with me might not be such a bad thing." He looked down at Ellie. "For both of you."

He backed out through the door, then reached up and touched a panel in the hall. The door slid shut.

Lian sat heavily on the bed. She could feel the panic building in her. Ellie tightened her grip and looked up at Lian with her big blue eyes. Her ears were clamped tight against the sides of her head.

"It's going to be okay," Lian said, stroking Ellie's back. "Nuar will find us. He'll come."

She hugged Ellie tight, willing her words to be true.

Chapter Fifteen

"This is taking too long!" Nuar strode across the common room and struck the wall as hard as he could. Light rippled out from the impact, a beautiful iridescent sheen that did nothing to comfort him.

"Our scans aren't detecting anything," Bron said. "Are you sure she's here?"

"Yes," Nuar said. "I know she's close. I can feel her. I just can't tell exactly where."

He looked at the holodisplay again. Gridlines divided the nearby space into quadrants that they had been searching for what felt like hours. Nothing had turned up.

Sometimes, Nuar felt as though he could sense Lian moving, but whenever Rom managed to get the *Arrow* to the new site they would find nothing.

"Whoever took her had to have been in a small ship to leave Earth undetected by the Vegans," Lar said.

Bron shrugged. "That assumes the Vegans can see through whatever cloak they're using."

If the Vegans couldn't see through this cloak... Nuar couldn't think of the ramifications of that. It would drive him insane.

His spine plates had been sticking straight out from his back, giving off waves of vibration in an irritating hum since they'd passed Mars. He'd torn the flimsy Earth shirt from his chest after it split from the pressure.

"We can't cover enough area to box him in," Bron said. "Even with our fighters, we would need at least two other vessels like the *Arrow* to have a chance at catching him."

Lar brought up a data feed. "The nearest Cygnian ships are two Earth days away through blue space transit."

"Two days?" Nuar shouted.

"Calm yourself," Lar said. "You've been able to track her this far. We won't lose our quarry."

"What if their ship can drop into blue space?" Nuar asked. "We have no idea what the range of my bond with Lian is. We have to act quickly before we lose her forever."

"We won't lose her," Bron said. "Cygnians don't fail."

"This isn't a battle we can force our way through," Nuar yelled.

"What do you suggest?" Lar asked.

"We could call the *Reckoning*," Nuar said.

"You would ask Sadirians for help?" Bron snorted dismissively.

"I would ask *anyone* for help." Nuar turned to Kral. "You came to Earth looking for your soulmate. Don't let me lose mine. Please."

Kral shook his head. "Cygnians do not ask other

sentients for help. We help each other. It's always been enough."

"And our people are dying out," Nuar said. "At the current rate of reproduction, we have only a few generations before we'll go extinct."

"Even if we find soulmates among Earthlings, that won't change anything," Bron said. "We're not biologically compatible."

Nuar turned to him. "Lian gives me hope. We can find a way to have children together. Or adopt and teach our children of Cygnian ways. At least our culture won't die with us."

"We walk a fine line here," Kral said. "My father has not authorized our presence in the Sol system."

"As if his approval has ever stopped you from doing what you want," Nuar said.

Kral held up a hand to silence him. "The stakes have never been so high. Not for us as a prism or as individual Cygnian warriors. Not for our people."

"Then think of our people," Nuar said. "Think of me. Think of the future for us all. I'm telling you, our future lies with Earth."

Kral held Nuar's gaze, his orange eyes gleaming. He looked back at the holodisplay—at the blank grids and the vast emptiness of space beyond.

"Lar," Kral said. "Connect me to Azure."

"You can't be serious," Lar said.

"Do it," Kral snapped.

"The Vegans have made it clear that their priority is Earth," Nuar said. "What if they won't help us?"

"An Earthling has been taken." Kral nodded. "They'll help."

A light flickered in the common room. Azure appeared. The holodisplay of the Vegan made it look as if she was on the ship with them.

"Kral," Azure said. "You have much to explain."

Kral arched a brow. "I wasn't aware that I had to tell you whenever I wished to leave Earth."

Azure held up a hand, gesturing to someone they couldn't see in the projection field. She must have another communication feed going.

"Your departure coincided with some disturbing disappearances." The sibilance of her voice grew more pronounced.

"We know Lian is missing," Nuar said. "Who else is gone? They must be the ones who took her."

"A male named Gary Simms can not be located," Azure said.

"Gary." Nuar's claws extended fully. He would rip out Gary's heart and crush it beneath his feet.

"We had hoped perhaps Gary and Lian were with you," Azure said.

"We left the planet in pursuit," Kral said. "We've been tracking Lian, but can't pinpoint her location."

"That is most unfortunate," Azure said. "She was not the only one taken."

"Who else?" Kral asked.

A crackling mass of light appeared—someone forcing their way into the connection. The holodisplay glitched a few times before coalescing into a huge white form that seemed to fill half the common room.

"Craig?" Nuar said.

The Lyrian's fur was standing out from his body in sharp points, making him look twice as big. He also had pulled himself to his full height—which Nuar corrected to at least eight feet. Craig's jaw had shifted forward, his serrated teeth prominently displayed.

"Lian was watching Ellie when she was taken," Craig said, his voice so distorted Nuar could hardly understand him. But when he parsed through the words, both his hearts beat even more urgently.

"The nestling?" Nuar said.

Kral stepped forward. "We had no idea."

Craig stalked to Kral, towering over him. "If I find that you are lying, Cygnian, I will rip you into tiny pieces, run them through my ship's power core, and then feed your remains to Barbara."

"This bickering and posturing does nothing to return our lost loved ones," Azure said. She turned to Nuar. "How are you tracking Lian?"

Before Nuar could respond, Lar said, "Nuar gave her

his wristbands."

It was true, but that wasn't how they were tracking Lian. Somehow, Gary was blocking the signal from the Cygnian tech. If she hadn't bonded with Nuar as his soulmate, there would be no way for them to track her.

The thought made Nuar sick with dread. Though she was angry at how quickly they had bonded, Nuar would be forever grateful for it.

"Send them all of our data," Kral said.

Lar stared at him instead of immediately complying. Nuar didn't miss the challenge in Lar's gaze.

"The *data*," Kral yelled.

With a low growl, Lar turned back to the communications station and began to work. Nuar was certain he'd be leaving out any mention of the soulmate bond.

"We will arrive in five minutes," Azure said, walking through Craig's holoprojection and disrupting the field. Craig reappeared in his original spot, still glowering at everyone.

"Five?" Bron said. "That's an impressive speed for intra-solar transit."

"We left Earth not long after you did," Azure said. "Though originally, we set out to stop Craig and Barbara from destroying your ship."

"*We* will arrive in *three* minutes," Craig said, peeling his lips further away from his teeth.

Azure snapped her fingers and two males flickered into the images crowding the room. One of them was tall, with light brown hair, blue eyes, and a strangely blank expression. Nuar recognized him as Marq, commander of the *Reckoning*.

Nuar had never thought he'd be grateful to see a Sadirian. He would take any help he could get.

The other man, Nuar didn't recognize. He was a little over six-feet tall, had short dark hair, dark eyes, and tanned skin. Something about his eyes unnerved Nuar, and he found himself becoming even more alert.

"Zemanni," Azure said. "Report."

"My ship isn't detecting any vessels in the area aside from the *Arrow*," he said. "But there's an interesting disruption in the transient substrate of this sector of space."

"Transient... What?" Lar asked.

Zemanni smirked at him. "Don't worry, Cygnian. We'll find something for you to hit any moment now."

Lar snarled and took a step toward the hologram. Kral grabbed his elbow and held him back.

"Who do you think you are?" Lar said.

"I'm the person who's been right on your back for the last half hour with none of you noticing," Zemanni said. "I'm the guy who's *already* here."

Not many ships had stealth fields the Cygnians couldn't see through. Lyrians were one.

Scorpiians were another.

"I heard rumors the Department of Homeworld Security was working with a Scorpiian," Kral said.

"You didn't think they were true?" Zemanni asked.

"I didn't think they were naive enough to risk it," Kral said.

"Enough." Azure stepped between them. "Zemanni has proven he will assist us. *You* have not."

"We will," Nuar said. He looked to Kral and repeated, "We will."

Kral nodded. "You have our cooperation."

"Well, then," Azure said. "Our priority is the retrieval of the missing sentients. If you would reactivate your holodisplay of this sector."

Bron input the command, and an additional holodisplay formed, showing the area they were searching.

"I see from the data you have sent us that you've narrowed the field of possibility to this section." Azure walked closer to the display and held up her small hands to show the area.

"If they even know what they're talking about," Zemanni said.

Azure cocked her head to the side and blinked her golden eyes at him. "You have a concern?"

"I've been following them since they reached Mars's orbit," Zemanni said. "Their path has been erratic. They've altered course at least three dozen times."

But only because Gary had altered *his*.

Every time their quarry changed his direction, they had changed theirs to follow. Though they could find his general area, they had no way to box him in—even with their personal fighters. Shards were designed to destroy, not take prisoners.

"Even so, they have been able to lead us to an area where you are detecting an anomaly," Azure said.

Zemanni shrugged.

Azure turned back to them. "Zemanni's point bears scrutiny. How have you been able to track this vessel when not even our Vegan sensors can see through it?"

Kral's back stiffened. Nuar could see his spine plates begin to rise beneath his shirt.

Before Nuar could intervene, Marq spoke up.

"The Cygnians are not part of our alliance," Marq said. "We have no right to ask them to divulge information that might put their people at risk."

The Sadirian's voice had the flat cadence of a soldier who had long had their emotions suppressed. Nuar actually felt a surge of sympathy for the man.

"Are we not allies in this mission?" Azure said, turning to Marq.

"We are working toward the same purpose," Marq said. "There's a difference. And the Cygnians have little at stake here. We owe them our gratitude for bringing us this far. They owe us nothing."

It was hard to believe a Sadirian would say such a thing on anyone else's behalf. It was also hard to believe he could be so wrong.

For Nuar, everything was at stake. And even if they didn't realize it yet, everything was on the line for the other warriors as well. For all of their people.

If they messed this up, Cygnians faced the chance of being banned from the Sol system. Banned from Earth. Nuar was sure that if that happened, his people's doom would be sealed.

"To find the path to a new future, there must often be a leap of faith," Nuar said. He was speaking as much to Kral and the rest of the prism as the sentients being projected into the room. "Perhaps this partnership will lay the foundation for an alliance in the future."

"Nuar," Lar snapped.

Kral held up a hand to silence the other warrior.

"Nuar's words are sound," Kral said. "I can't promise that my mother will sanction an official alliance, but I can promise that I and my prism will do everything in our power to return Lian and the nestling safely to their families."

Azure regarded him for a few moments, then nodded.

"Very well," she said. "We shall place our faith in you." She narrowed her eyes at Kral. "Do not disappoint us."

Chapter Sixteen

"I am a stubborn idiot."

Lian sat on the bed leaning against the wall. Her knees were pulled up so that Ellie could rest against them as they stared at each other.

Lian held one set of Ellie's hands and wiggled her arms they way the little Lyrian liked. The nestling's tentacles were still holding tight to Lian's sides. She could tell that Ellie was scared.

So was Lian.

"It's okay," Lian said. "Nuar will come for us."

She didn't know how she knew. She just did.

She could feel him out there. Somewhere close. He was searching for her.

"Storming out was not the smartest thing I've ever done in my life," she said. "I should have stayed and asked more questions."

Light caught on the shining wristbands she wore. "I could have at least asked him how to use these things."

For all she knew, they had weapons and shields and distress calls or something that could help get them out of this mess.

It didn't matter if they did. Lian had no idea how to activate them.

She imagined what it would have been like if she'd asked Nuar about the wristbands. He would have teased her as he taught her. She would have glared a lot—as always. But he would have laughed and kissed her till she couldn't think straight.

That's what life with him would be like. She was sure of it. And the more she thought about it, the more she wanted that life.

She wanted someone who wasn't scared off by her moods. Someone who didn't back down when she was mad at them. Someone who loved her because of who she was—not in spite of it.

Nuar was her soulmate. Now that she'd had time to think, she knew it was true. She could feel it. She'd been able to all along, if she was honest with herself.

No one had ever gotten to her the way he did. No one got under her skin.

Except Nuar. Because he was already there. Part of her soul that she hadn't realized was missing.

If he didn't find her, she and Ellie were heading for a laboratory. Lian wrapped her arms around Ellie and hugged her close.

What would they do to the nestling? How could Lian possibly protect her?

She should never have agreed to babysit. If Ellie had

been with Craig or Barbara, Gary couldn't have taken her. He'd said so himself.

This was Lian's fault.

No it isn't.

The voice in her head sounded like Nuar. She looked up, almost thinking she'd see him there, even though she knew he wasn't in the room. She could still feel the distance between them. It was just wishful thinking.

That didn't mean she couldn't enjoy it.

She rested her cheek on the top of Ellie's head and closed her eyes, imagining that Nuar was in the room. Wondering what he'd say.

This is Gary's fault and his alone. He's the one who kidnapped you.

But Lian was the one who had run off.

And if you hadn't? Gary was waiting for a chance to take Ellie. If he hadn't taken you with her, he would have taken someone else. Or taken her alone.

Okay, Nuar-in-her-head had a point. Lian wasn't the only one who babysat Ellie. Sometimes, Olivia would watch the little Lyrian.

The idea of one of her best friends being taken along with Ellie was too much. Lian's eyes filled with tears again.

Lian had been taken, and she was a Cygnian soulmate. Nuar could find her. He *would* find her. She was sure of it.

If one of her friends had been taken instead... Lian

squeezed Ellie tighter, shying away from that line of thinking.

What she needed to do was figure out how to help Nuar. The trouble was, she didn't have any weapons or fighting skill.

She would fix that after Nuar rescued her. Learn to be a warrior. Challenge him to battle to claim him as her husband—and beat him.

Somehow.

The door to the room slid open. Gary stood on the other side.

"Hello, Lian," he said. "I hope you were able to get a bit of rest."

"Fuck you."

"You should watch your language around the nestling."

"Uck," Ellie said. "Uckoo."

Oh crap.

Gary had the gall to laugh. "See?"

Lian knew she couldn't set fire to him with her eyes. She tried anyway.

"When you're done glaring at me, could you join me in the command room?" he asked.

She wanted to say, "When Hell freezes over," but Ellie was still saying, "Uckoo," over and over.

Lian really hoped that wasn't Ellie's first word.

"I should have thought that through," Gary said. "You'll never be done glaring. I need you in command.

Now."

"Give me one reason I should do anything to help you."

"I'm about to call your boyfriend."

Her heart leapt into her throat.

"Nuar?" she asked.

"Unless you have a different Cygnian boyfriend?"

She scowled, not wanting to cooperate, but desperate to see Nuar again.

Dammit.

She slid off the bed.

"Excellent," Gary said. He stepped back so she could walk past him into the narrow corridor, gesturing toward the room she'd seen earlier at the end of the hall.

The command room was more spacious than the room that served as her cell. The walls were rounded, making it feel like she was walking inside a giant ball as she crossed the floor to the center of the room. Even the ceiling was curved.

She could make out panels on some spots of the walls, with buttons and etchings and flashing lights—none of which Lian had the faintest idea how to use. She glanced around, hoping for something like an emergency exit.

Right. An exit into space. Like that would be a good idea.

An escape pod would be nice, though.

Gary tapped a few of the buttons on his bracer. The

walls surrounding them were replaced with a field of stars. The dark flooring blended in, making her feel as if she was standing in the middle of outer space.

Lian's breath caught in her chest. It was absolutely beautiful—and terrifying. All she could see was blackness and stars.

Until she turned around.

Floating in the middle of the void was a huge crystal. It was milky-white with iridescent rainbow patterns rippling across its surface, like a moonstone. Even without something for scale, Lian had the sense that it was huge.

Lights flickered behind her. When she turned, she saw that a monitor had appeared on one of the walls, superimposed over the backdrop of space. Kral was pictured in the center of the screen, his orange eyes glowing bright. Nuar stood just behind his shoulder.

Lian took a step forward instinctively. Nuar's eyes widened when he saw her.

The room they were in looked like it was the same milky-white as the huge crystal. Did that mean it was their ship?

Gary bowed slightly. "Greetings, Kral."

"Give us your prisoners," Kral demanded.

"Not one for formalities, I guess," Gary said.

Ellie took that moment to chime in with, "Uckoo!"

Lian held the nestling closer against her chest.

"There are no prisoners on this ship," Gary said. "Only

test subjects."

Nuar's eyes widened, their red irises gleaming like lasers. He shoved Kral aside.

"I will rip your limbs from your body and beat you to death with them," Nuar yelled.

Lian would watch. She'd probably cover Ellie's eyes, though.

"Interesting," Gary said. "I might be persuaded to return Lian to you, but only if you explain how you've managed to follow me."

A muscle in Nuar's cheek twitched.

"Not even the Vegans can see through this cloak," Gary went on. "And yet, your ship followed perfectly, no matter how many times I changed course."

"Then you know you can't escape us," Kral said.

Gary laughed. "When I realized you were tracking me, I set up a series of tests to see how accurate your sensors are. I know you can tell my general vicinity, but you can't predict where I'm going and you certainly can't stop me from leaving."

"You think so?" Kral said, a menacing note in his voice.

Gary smirked. "The ship's engines have only been at half capacity."

Kral's brow furrowed and his eyes ramped up their own glow.

"Is it the wristbands?" Gary asked. "I was thinking

about removing them so I could toss them out an airlock, just in case. I'd love to examine their technology, but it's more important that I figure out this flaw in the ship's cloak."

Nuar snorted. "You can't remove them. You don't know how."

"Of course I do," Gary said. "They're attached to her wrists. I simply remove her wrists."

This time, Lian snorted. "They're kind of attached to my arms, dumbass."

Gary turned toward her with a dispassionate stare. "For the moment."

She felt like ice had flooded her veins. He couldn't be serious, could he?

Gary started tapping more commands on his bracer. A short, thin line of intense yellow light projected from the top of it. The bulky bracer made a high-pitched humming sound.

He started walking toward Lian, and said, "Don't worry. The laser will cauterize the injury. I can even deaden the pain, if you promise to cooperate."

Lian hugged Ellie tighter and took a step back.

"Sadirian scum!" Nuar yelled. "Harm her, and I'll throw you into Cygnus X to let the black hole rip you apart atom by atom."

Gary turned back to the screen. "You can't get signals through my shielding. If you could activate her wristbands' defenses, you wouldn't be so panicked. That's interesting. It's logical to assume if the shielding blocks signals from one direction, it also blocks them from the other."

"What?" Lian asked, her heart racing as she kept staring at the laser-like light coming from his bracer.

Gary followed her gaze and smiled. He tapped a button on his bracer and the light vanished.

"The wristbands aren't what they're tracking," Gary said. "You can keep your hands for a while longer. Of course, if your boyfriend tells me how to remove the wristbands without harming you, you could remain intact for the foreseeable future. Once we get to the base, my colleagues are going to want a closer look at them."

"I have another suggestion," Kral said. The corner of his mouth pulled up in a smile. "Return Lian and Ellie to us unharmed and I promise you a quick end."

"Cygnians love to make threats," Gary said. "But one ship is—"

Kral interrupted. "Who said I only have one ship?"

A beeping sound filled the room. Gary's mouth dropped open as he slowly turned, staring at the view of space all around them.

As Lian looked as well, ships winked into view. A cream colored, nautilus-looking ship that was four times the size of Nuar's appeared off to her left. A small, angular ship straight out of a scifi movie—perfect for space fights and racing through atmospheres—was to her right. Superimposed behind the screen in front of them was a large, cylindrical ship with a gunmetal gray hull that she could barely make out next to the backdrop of space, even after it dropped its cloak.

Gary slowly turned back to the monitor where Kral was openly smirking. Behind him, Nuar's brow was still pinched with worry as he stared at Lian.

"I'm surprised," Gary said.

"What, that the Cygnian crown prince asked for help?" Kral asked, a bit of a growl in his voice.

"No," Gary said. "That they answered. There's a wonderful Earth expression: 'You have to be a friend to have a friend.' The Cygnians aren't exactly known for being…outgoing."

"Things change," Kral said.

"Indeed, they do." Gary smiled. "But not quite enough, I think. Four vessels can't box me in."

"Again, you underestimate my *friends*." Kral sneered a bit as he said the word.

Lian wondered why, until she saw four flying saucers ripple into view above them. She knew those ships. Sadirian interceptors.

From the sound of the renewed beeping, Lian wouldn't be surprised if there were more below, where the view was blocked.

"*Sadirians?*" Gary said, his voice filled with disbelief.

"You would work with the Coalition?"

He turned back to Lian. "What is so special about you that they would do this? That Kral himself would stand alongside the same Sadirians who experimented on his sister for decades?"

"The way I see it, the only sadistic Sadirian here is standing in front of me," Kral said.

Gary laughed. "I suppose you'd see it that way."

"You have nowhere to run," Kral said.

Gary was quiet for a few moments. Something about his calm demeanor was actually freaking Lian out more than anything she'd seen or heard so far.

"Sadirians, you don't have to do this," Gary said, a sudden strength entering his tone. He looked around at the ships surrounding them. "The High Council will take care of you. They'll take care of everyone, as they always have."

"The High Council has been destroyed," Kral said.

Gary continued as if Kral hadn't spoken. "Things don't have to be like this. Chaotic and uncertain. The High Council will restore order. Help me and you'll see."

Lian could barely breathe. She knew there were factions within the Sadirians that were still loyal to the High Council and that they hadn't all been reached yet. Gary was proof of that.

But the High Council was gone—and it was a good thing. How could anyone want to return to being controlled and programmed like a machine?

The interceptors started to move away.

It was like a blow to the chest. All of them were leaving... Except, they stopped when they were perfectly equidistant from each other. The interceptors shifted to different angles so that their flat undersides pointed at Gary's ship. Beams of white light shot out from one ship to another. The light formed a web-like net surrounding Gary's ship.

Lian let out a laugh that was closer to a sob. She hugged Ellie as tight as she could. They were going to be okay.

"I guess they've chosen their side," Lian said.

Gary looked all around them, then said, "Apparently so."

He opened his mouth and then closed it again, as if he wanted to say something, but was unsure of himself. His face paled, and she could see him work to swallow. When he turned to her, he looked nervous for the first time since she'd known him.

"Dean isn't going to like this," he said.

"Wait, the Scorpiian?" Lian asked. "He's behind this?"

Gary didn't respond, but his lips thinned.

"We can protect you from him," Lian said. "We'll keep you safe."

Gary gave a mirthless laugh. "No one is safe from him. He's the High Council's right hand. Now and always. He chose me to help him with this and I've failed. I've failed the High Council."

"There's still time," Lian said. "You don't have to hold on to their programming."

He smiled up at her. "But I want to. Dean chose me. I want to help. There's only one thing left that I can do."

He ran his fingers through his hair, then took a deep breath and let it out. He turned toward the main viewscreen, then lifted his bracer and tapped in a few commands.

He paused, his hand hovering over a blinking red light. Something about that lingering moment filled her with renewed dread.

He looked at her over his shoulder, his smile wistful.

"I really did like you," he said.

"Gary, wait!" she screamed. But it was too late.

He tapped his bracer, then closed his eyes.

The room erupted into flames. Lian dropped into a crouch, wrapping as much of herself around Ellie as she could, even though she knew it was futile. She had one last glimpse of Gary before the explosion engulfed him.

Lian clenched her eyes shut. She could still see light flickering behind her eyelids.

Oh, Ellie. I'm so sorry...

Lian held her breath. Everything felt suspended, like time itself had stopped. She waited for the pain and heat to hit her. Something soft slapped her face instead. She opened one eye, then another.

Ellie was staring up at her, chewing on her fingers. She poked Lian's face again with one of her tentacles.

They were floating in space. All around them, scraps of twisted metal floated in an eerie, suspended landscape. Everything was gold-tinged.

Why aren't we dead?

She tried to say something comforting to Ellie, but no sound came out. It felt like there was something covering her mouth—her entire body. It tingled a bit, like the field Nuar had used while they were "bonding."

She should probably conserve oxygen anyway. Where was it coming from?

There was air around her, but only just next to her skin. She could feel it sliding over her cheeks as she breathed in and out.

A large hunk of debris floated past her, clearing more of her view. Before her, she could see the Cygnian ship, beautifully backlit against the stars. Her eyes filled with tears as she thought of Nuar so close and yet out of reach.

Except...

A hatch opened in the side of the ship. Nuar gripped the sides of the opening. He flung himself forward, arms outstretched, heading straight for Lian and Ellie.

He wasn't wearing a spacesuit or anything. He didn't even have on a shirt.

The spines running down his back were standing bolt

upright and he was staring at her with more intensity than she'd ever seen. His eyes were glowing bright red.

Please catch us... Please catch us...

As he drew closer, she could see a golden glow surrounding him, just above his skin. Was it an energy field?

It was the same gold that had been tinging everything in her view since the ship exploded. She wondered if she was in one of those, too.

Nuar spread his arms just before reaching her, then wrapped them around her and Ellie both, drawing them against his chest.

Lian burrowed her face against him. A weird energy crackled over her skin. She felt tears flowing down her face and for once, she didn't care.

She was in Nuar's arms. She and Ellie were safe. And that was all that mattered.

Chapter Seventeen

Nuar's hearts were pounding, even with Lian and Ellie in his arms. He wouldn't breathe easy until they were aboard the Lyrian ship.

Though their momentum had lessened, they kept moving along in the same direction Nuar had initiated when he leapt from the *Arrow*. Craig and Barbara's ship was straight ahead.

Bursts of light flickered as Barbara fired the ship's thrusters minimally, lining up to receive the group floating toward the Lyrian ship. The main hatch opened, and Craig pulled himself into view. He clung to the sides of the hatch with his toes, then spread all four arms, ready to catch them even if they weren't quite on target.

Lian craned her neck around so she could see where they were heading. Nuar felt a shudder of relief pass through her when she saw Craig waiting for them. Nuar hugged her tighter as she turned back and buried her face against his chest.

The Lyrian nestling squirmed and he eased up a bit. Ellie looked up at him and smiled, wrapping a tentacle around his arm and holding tight.

Thank the stars Nuar had been able to activate the force field in Lian's wristbands the moment Gary's shields had gone down. There had only been a split second between that moment and the destruction of his ship.

Feeling Lian's panic had spurred Nuar to action. He wasn't sure he could have timed it so perfectly without their connection.

He never, ever, wanted to test that out again.

It seemed to take an eternity, but they finally came within Craig's reach. The Lyrian grabbed Nuar and pulled the whole bundle of sentients tight against him, reaching with his one free hand to grab the side of the hatch and help to pull them back into the ship.

The hatch closed and the airlock filled with breathable atmosphere. Lights filtered through the small space, completing decontamination procedures.

Nuar couldn't bring himself to let go of Lian. Not even to deactivate the force field that had saved her and Ellie's lives. He held her as she shuddered against him, at once cursing and blessing the shields that crackled between them.

"Excuse me," Craig said. "You need to deactivate those shields. We want to hold our nestling and Barbara is losing her patience."

Lian smiled up at Nuar. He finally managed to push away from her enough to strike his wristbands together and hum the notes that would deactivate both of their fields. Ellie wriggled between them, her tentacles and arms reaching for Craig as she babbled to him.

She gripped Craig's neck tight and started saying, "Uckoo! Uckoo!"

Lian grimaced.

"What's that, little one?" Craig asked, keeping all four of his hands on the nestling as if he couldn't bring himself to let go.

Nuar knew the feeling. He pulled Lian closer to his chest.

"Uh, it's just some gibberish thing she picked up," Lian said. "I have no idea where."

Craig nodded, looking Ellie over like he was making sure all her parts were still there. He turned toward the bridge when Lian called out to him.

"Craig," she said. "I'm so sorry. I tried to protect Ellie as best I could."

Nuar felt a surge of pride at his mate's courage. And yet, she seemed to be berating herself over something.

"Gary's ship..." A shudder passed over her again. "I couldn't stop him. If it hadn't been for Nuar—"

Craig snorted. "Nuar saved *you*. And I'm glad for that. But Ellie wasn't in danger from the ship exploding. Even as a nestling, Lyrians are nearly indestructible."

He stroked Ellie's head, his hand stilling on her back as he bent his forehead to hers.

"But taking her..." Craig's voice cracked in a way

Nuar didn't know a Lyrian's could. He looked back at Lian. "The universe is a very big place. I don't know if we could have ever found her again."

Craig surprised Nuar by pulling both him and Lian into a hug, two of his arms holding them close as the other pair held onto Ellie. He leaned down and pressed his forehead to Lian's and then to Nuar's.

"Thank you for returning my daughter to me," Craig said. He released them after another moment, then turned and walked away.

"Lian—" Nuar said.

Before he could say more, she threw her arms around his neck and pulled herself to his lips to kiss him.

The moment their mouths touched, he was lost. A flame of need burst through his body. He crushed his lips to hers, his tongue sliding within, renewing his claim. She raked her fingers through his hair, shifting her body closer.

Nuar let his hands slide to her ass and lifted her from her feet. She wrapped her legs around his waist, pressing her hips against his stomach. He walked them to the corridor's wall, pinning her against it and grinding against her core.

He needed to be inside of her. Needed to feel her clenching around him, screaming his name.

"Do not mate on my ship!" Craig's voice boomed from down the corridor. "Ellie is too young to be smelling that. Honestly."

They broke off the kiss and laughed. Nuar felt more of his tension ease.

He kissed her once more—he couldn't help it—but gently this time. He let his hands rove over her back, reassuring himself that she was in one piece. She was safe and she was whole.

Her hands were doing much the same to him. They reached his highest spine, curiously exploring the texture.

He moaned and said, "If you keep doing that, I may risk the Lyrian's wrath and take you against this wall."

"We probably shouldn't," Lian said. "It's bad enough that I taught Ellie a swear word."

Lian released her grip with her legs and Nuar lowered her to her feet. She wrapped her arms around his chest and pressed herself against him, as if she still couldn't get close enough.

Feeling her need—sharing it—he held her closer.

"I was afraid I'd never see you again," she said.

"I feared the same thing."

After a pause, she said, "I'm not sorry I ran off."

"Nor should you be. I… I got everything wrong. I didn't understand your ways and how different we are. I didn't realize how much you didn't know about Cygnians. But I promise you, I'll dedicate myself to studying your culture so that I don't mess up again."

She laughed, the sound reassuring him more than he thought possible.

"I'm sure we'll both mess up plenty," she said. "We'll need to learn to forgive and support each other if we're going to spend the rest of our lives together."

His hearts started pounding. Was she accepting him? Embracing their bond?

"You don't mind that we're bonded?" he asked. "You don't regret it?"

His breath stilled as he waited for her answer.

"You were able to find us because of our bond, weren't you?" she said.

"I was."

She was quiet for long enough that the room seemed to spin. He didn't think he could breathe again until he knew her answer.

She leaned back and looked up at him, her eyes bright with tears that she blinked away.

"Craig told me that most things happen for the right reason and at the right time, even if we don't understand it," she said. "I'm so glad everything happened between us the way it did—and when it did. I don't regret anything. I want to learn more. I want to learn everything. About us. About our bond. About you."

His chest felt as if it would burst. The spines along his back quivered, lighting up the space with rainbow patterns. Lian laughed as she looked around, wonder clear upon her lovely features.

"I want to learn, too," Nuar said. "And I'll need your

help. My people have a lot to adapt to if we're going to become more active among other sentients."

Lian turned her head to look out the hatch's viewport. Beyond it, the Vegan ship could still be seen, as well as the interceptors collecting the remains of Gary's ship.

"It looks like you'll have plenty of support," she said.

She was right. For the first time, the Cygnians weren't acting alone in the universe.

His hearts filled with an emotion he hadn't felt for his people in a long time.

Hope.

Chapter Sixteen

Once they reached the *Arrow*, Lian could barely contain her excitement. She was in space. She had been on not one, but *two* spaceships.

Three if she counted Gary's.

Which she didn't.

"I had no idea your wristbands could do so many awesome things," she said. "What else can they do? Rayguns? Lasers? Connect to the Internet?"

Nuar laughed. "First of all, those are *your* wristbands. I have a new pair." He lifted his free arm, showing her one of the bands of gleaming metal wrapped around his wrists.

She had a death grip on his other arm and was not about to let go of it. Well, maybe if he wanted to wrap it around her she could be convinced.

"Great," she said. "Then what can *my* wristbands do?"

"I'll teach you, but not quite yet."

She scowled. It felt more like a pout than a glare. What was this guy doing to her?

A better question was, what was he *planning* to do with her?

A jolt of pleasure shot to her core as she realized they

were back on his ship, where he presumably had a bed. She hadn't slept with him in a bed yet. Or not slept with him in a bed.

"Well, when you start, the first thing I want to know is how to activate that force field/oxygen generator thing," she said. "That is incredibly useful."

"It works underwater, too," Nuar said.

Her eyes widened. "No way."

Nuar laughed.

"What do we need to do first?" she said, leaning closer and rising on her toes as they walked. Damn, her man was tall.

"We need to talk to the others."

"Oh." She dropped back down onto her heels.

"You had something else in mind?" he asked.

"I had *several* something elses in mind."

Finally picking up on her queues, he paused. She could feel his desire rolling off of him, even though their bond was new.

Apparently, they had to be really worked up to feel each other's emotions at the moment. As the years went on, he assured her they'd be able to sense more of each other—and learn to block it when they wanted to, which was a big relief.

Lian could get...cranky. At least she was self-aware about it.

"Not now, Cygnian," she said, pulling on his arm and

heading forward. "Apparently, we have people to talk to."

"As quickly as possible," he muttered.

She laughed as he scooped her up against his side, leading her into a spacious room. A spacious, but very full room.

There were so many people.

Marq, commander of the *Reckoning*. Azure and another Vegan Lian didn't know. Some hot human or Sadirian-looking guy with dark hair.

And the entire prism was there, milling among the others and looking vaguely uncomfortable and entirely menacing. When each of them looked at Lian, their expressions morphed into happiness and welcome.

It was so weird.

Kral reached her first. He plucked her from Nuar's side and lifted her in a huge hug.

"Lian!" he said. "We're so glad you're safe."

Another Cygnian, one with indigo eyes and almost purplish-blue skin, took her from Kral and gave her a hug before setting her on her feet. She was pretty sure that was Tarn.

"Don't suffocate the Earthling," he said. "They're fragile."

"Not this one!" Another Cygnian—who had to be Rom, with those gorgeous violet eyes—pulled her into a hug, but it wasn't quite as...enthusiastic as Kral's. "She could scare the scales off a quryl with that glare of hers."

Lian gave him a good dose of one when he set her down. Nancy was going to die of jealousy when Lian told her friends about this.

Lian heard a low woof, then Ed came bounding up to her. Well, it was more of a quick shamble, but that was what he did when he was excited. She dropped to her knees and wrapped her arms around her dog as he licked her face, his tail wagging like crazy.

"What are you doing here?" Lian asked. "Are you in space? Are you a space doggie?" She glanced up at the Cygnians surrounding her, all of whom had a mixture of curiosity and amusement lighting their features. She laughed, and said, "Seriously, why is Ed here?"

"You told me to watch over him, so I brought him with me," Nuar said.

"I guess that makes sense." She stood, keeping one hand in Ed's ruff.

"Excuse us." Craig waved an arm over his head.

Rom stepped away from Lian, joining a cobalt-skinned warrior with golden eyes and another with green who was built like a brick wall. Lar and Bron. She was going to have to practice remembering all their names.

"Lian!" Craig said, extending all four arms.

She went to hug him, but passed right through his body, stumbling to keep her footing. Ed barked, then trotted over to a bench built into one of the walls and laid down beneath it.

"Oops," Craig said. "I forgot I'm not really here." He looked around. "I have to say, you Cygnians really do know your way around a hologram."

"It helps when your planet is all about light and crystals," Nuar said, coming to stand at Lian's side. "You okay?"

She nodded. "Yeah. I guess I need to check that people are actually in the room before I try to hug them."

"Sorry about that," Craig said. "I will give you the biggest hug ever once we're in the same room. You know. Physically."

"And so will I." Barbara stepped out from behind Craig, holding little Ellie. The Lyrian reached out and Lian had to remind herself yet again that the nestling wasn't actually in the room with them.

"Now, now," Barbara said. "You can play with Lian when we get back to Earth. But I must say, I don't think I'll be able to let you out of my sight for a while."

The backs of Lian's eyes started to burn again. "Barbara, I'm so sorry."

"For what?" Barbara stood up straighter, bringing her to about Craig's armpit.

From what Lian had heard, Barbara had been taller than Craig until recently. Some sort of incident had caused her to go into stasis, which made her lose a bunch of mass and shrink. After hearing what Craig said about Ellie surviving a ship exploding, Lian had to wonder what the hell had happened to cause that.

"You have nothing to apologize for," Barbara said.

"I was the one watching Ellie when she was taken," Lian said.

Barbara snorted. "You protected my offspring."

"Not that I could do much," Lian mumbled.

"Gary was intent on taking my nestling from me." Barbara held one of Ellie's hands and wiggled her arm. "I thank the Makers that you were with her when it happened."

"But—" Lian began, thinking of all the people who could have handled it better.

"*You* were the one to walk away," Barbara said. "Not Gary. And you did it with my nestling. For that, I will be forever grateful."

Lian's vision blurred again. Barbara made a little clucking noise.

"Not in front of the males," she said. "It's bad enough that I'm this ridiculous size."

"You look menacing as always, my sweet," Craig said.

Barbara glared at him. Yeah, there was a reason Lian got along so well with the pair. She laughed, catching Barbara's attention again.

"Sorry," Lian said. "I was just thinking we should go on a double-date sometime."

She wrapped her arm around Nuar's waist and looked up at him with a smile. He returned it uneasily, then turned to Craig.

"Is it just me, or is the glare less unnerving?" Nuar said.

Lian poked him in the ribs. Which did absolutely nothing, except make him laugh.

"You'll grow accustomed to each other's moods," Craig said. "And learn to take delight in all of them. Mostly."

Barbara poked Craig in the ribs, as Lian had Nuar, and Craig laughed.

"Sweetling, you know I'm ticklish," he said.

Kral came over to them after talking to the Vegans. Marq crossed the room to join them as well, making Kral look profoundly uncomfortable.

"I would like to thank you for your assistance," Marq said.

"That's not necessary," Kral said.

"Really?" Craig crossed all four of his arms over his massive chest. "Because it seems to me that we wouldn't have been able to rescue our nestling and our friend without you."

"It really does." Barbara crossed two of her arms. The other pair were still busy with Ellie. "In fact, we should also be thanking you Cygnians."

Kral glanced over at Nuar. Lian wondered why they didn't just come out and say that she was Nuar's soulmate. From the sound of it, that was a big deal. Maybe such a big deal that they needed to keep it secret?

She would have to tell Nuar that Craig already knew. Later.

"If anyone is thanking anybody, it's me," Lian said. "I'm the one who was rescued. So, thanks. All of you."

"You're welcome," Barbara said.

"We're just glad we were in the right place at the right time." Craig winked at Lian.

She glared at him, and he laughed.

"If I may have your attention." All eyes turned to Azure as she stepped into the center of the quieting room.

"While we are delighted that our friends have been returned to us, these events bring matters of grave concern to our attention," she said. "Gary had a ship with a cloaking field well beyond any of our capabilities to detect."

She paused for a moment as that sunk in.

"Unfortunately, when he destroyed it, he removed our chance to study whatever technology it contained," she said. "I remind you that there is a war going on in the galaxy. One which we had believed to be between the Tau Centauran Assembly and the Sadirians of the Coalition of Planets. It would seem in that assumption we were mistaken." She turned to Marq and said, "Commander."

He stepped forward. "We have analyzed what little we could salvage from Gary's ship. It would seem to be of Centauran origins," Marq said. "Gary—a Sadirian who wishes to hold on to the ways of the High Council—was in possession of this ship. We must explore the possibility that there are other Sadirians working in concert with the Assembly."

"Given this knowledge, the Vegans must chose a different course of action," Azure said. "Our priority remains protecting Earth, our new homeworld. But it is no longer in our best interest to remain neutral and we cannot in good conscience do so."

Lian felt Nuar twitch next to her. Even Craig and Barbara stared at the Vegan in stunned silence.

"I cannot overstate the implications of this," Azure said. "The Assembly has access to technology that outstrips our own. We Vegans have not encountered this in…" She shook her head and her eyes took on a haunted quality. "Not since we left our own homeworld."

"What does this mean for us?" Barbara asked.

"It's simple." Lian interlaced her fingers with Nuar's and looked up at him. "It means we need to work together. All of us."

Kral joined Marq and Azure in the center of the room.

"We would like to return to Earth and explore the possibilities of…working together," Kral said.

"That is for the Earthlings to decide," Azure said. "Especially after the damages caused."

Lian felt a burst of panic. If the Cygnians were ordered to leave, what would happen with her and Nuar? Would she have to choose between her soulmate and her homeworld?

"Everyone makes mistakes," Lian said, speaking quickly. "If we can't learn to move past them, we'll never be able to work together. Besides, Nuar has to return to Earth to set things right in the greenhouse. He has to stay at least until the plants are back to the state they were in before he trashed them."

Nuar laughed as he put his arms around her and drew her against his chest. "That might take a while."

"I don't care if it takes a lifetime," she said.

Craig groaned. "Get a room."

"Actually, I do have a room aboard the ship," Nuar said.

"Does it have a bed?" Lian asked.

Azure's browridge rose. "With that, I will take my leave."

"I believe I will as well," Marq said. "I look forward to seeing you back on Earth and am glad to have moved forward on a path I hope will lead to friendship between all our peoples."

The holograms winked out, leaving the room quite a bit emptier, but still filled with huge blue guys. There was only one that held Lian's interest, though, and he was staring at her with smoldering red eyes.

"We need to speak of this with the queen," Lar said. "Steps must be taken."

"The only steps I'm interested in taking are to my quarters." Nuar bent down and lifted Lian into his arms.

She clung to his neck and said, "Yeah, we need more time to bond."

Laughing, Nuar carried her from the room and into a future she couldn't wait to explore.

Epilogue

Kral had never seen Nuar happier. He had seldom seen any Cygnian that happy. Then again, he'd rarely seen pairs of soulmates before, aside from his parents.

He longed for that bond. He felt the pull of it. At least, he thought he did.

It was not coming from Harbor.

The Department of Homeworld Security had asked him to wait for six months while they prepared for his arrival. Six months until he could visit their planet and track down the Earthling known as Becca.

The closest Kral could get to her was spending time with her brother, Buddy. Through him, he knew that their family held values he revered. Loyalty, trust, family, and friends.

He knew from Buddy that she was strong. She didn't trust easily, but she protected her loved ones fiercely once she did. He had coaxed stories from Buddy during their time together.

But Kral wanted to know *Becca*. He had to meet her. Especially now, when things on Earth were becoming ever more dangerous.

There was a war going on. A war that Earth was being drawn deeper into. It couldn't stay on the outskirts much longer.

Kral needed to be at Becca's side. He needed to protect her and for her to protect him.

They were a pair, fated to be together. She just didn't know it yet.

But she would.

Soon.

—

Thank you so much for reading *Nuar: A Scifi Alien Warriors Romance*, the first *Cygnian 7* novel! We are just getting started in this world, but there is plenty of adventure in store for you. Keep reading for a sneak peek at the second *Cygnian 7* novel, *Kral: A Scifi Alien Warriors Romance!*

Kral: A Scifi Alien Warriors Romance

Cygnian 7
Book Two

Chapter One

Family dinner night was not the time to be thinking of the maddening restlessness that was consuming Becca. Ever since Christmas, it had been growing in her—a strange sense of *something* that kept her awake at night.

She thought it might have something to do with Buddy announcing his first ever serious relationship to the family right around then. Settling down had never been high on her agenda. Her family always came first, and she'd never met a guy she felt was good enough to be part of that.

She'd always thought that was something she and Buddy had in common. Seeing him settle down made her start to think if maybe it was time for her to think about it, too. The idea of a house and a picket fence and a regular nine-to-five set her teeth on edge, though. That life was not for her.

The restlessness chose that moment to rise up in her almost irresistibly. She paused near the table, staring at the front door and imagining dropping everything and running outside. She wasn't sure where she'd be running to, though.

Or to who.

"Watch it," Amy said, ducking underneath the serving plate Becca was carrying into the dining room from the kitchen.

Amy wasn't just the youngest sibling—she was also the smallest, even though she was in her early twenties. She still had to bend over to miss the plate that was heaped high with Mom and Buddy's spectacular cooking. Dad was pouring drinks as the middle sister, Sophie put down the last of the utensils.

Shaken from whatever that was, Becca headed back to the table.

She wished they could do this more than once a month. Then again, as she surveyed the epic feast on the table, she realized what a massive undertaking that would be. It was a miracle their big family could coordinate their schedules, especially now that Buddy was so busy with Nika.

He barely even had time to help out with running his own business. Becca had needed to take over much of the management of his sub shop while he was off helping his girlfriend.

How was he even helping her? She was some kind of high-end mechanic or engineer or something.

"Excuse me." The man himself swept into the room with the main course, his apron stained from cooking.

Pickles and Dazzle, the family's two Pomeranians, danced around Buddy's ankles, their heads craned back to keep the dish in sight. They barked as if hoping they could startle a piece of meat into falling to the ground.

"Get," Becca said, waving the little orange fluff balls

away. "Go to your beds. Can't you be more like Dash?"

Sophie's border collie looked up from her bed, where she'd been lying in a civilized manner since Sophie instructed her to, a huge smile on her doggie face. Pickles let out a chuff, but both little dogs scurried away.

"Sophie, you're a professional dog trainer," Becca said. "You have to teach us what to do about these pom-poms."

Sophie shook her head. "I think they're beyond me."

Becca pushed some dishes aside to make room for the main dish. Roasted potatoes, carrots, parsnips, and onions surrounded the prime cut of meat. She took a deep breath, leaning over the dish and savoring the aromas.

"Buddy, this smells amazing," she said.

"Of course it does." He nodded, staring at the dish as if he was still looking for ways to improve it. He must not have found any, because he took off the oven mitts he'd been wearing and picked up the carving knives she'd laid out for him earlier.

The rest of the family hurried in, drawn by the scent, no doubt. Becca sat next to her mom at one end of the table, with her dad at the other end and Sophie and Amy across from her.

The conversation between her sisters and parents filled the room, along with the clatter of dishes. It was a nice distraction, but not enough to mask her agitation.

There was something she needed to do or somewhere she needed to go. Something was…missing.

One leg bounced under the table and goosebumps rose along her arms. The goosebumps flowed up to her neck, then down her spine. She hadn't known she could even get goosebumps there.

"I can't believe Hayley is missing this," Amy said, pulling Becca's attention back to the table. "Couldn't she have come home from her trip a few days early?"

"She knows we'll fill our fridge with leftovers." Sophie passed her plate to Buddy to get loaded up and the rest of the family followed suit.

"Or, you could just come here to eat them," Mom said. "It seems she's always traveling lately. We haven't seen enough of her since she came back from Paris."

"You and me both," Sophie murmured.

Hayley was Sophie's best friend and had practically grown up with her and Becca. She'd lost her parents way too early, and Sophie and Becca had moved in to her parent's house with her as soon as Becca finished high school. They still lived together, over a decade later, though Hayley was often gone with her work as a travel writer.

Something had happened in Paris that neither Sophie nor Hayley were talking about. It was yet another thing driving Becca crazy. How could she help them if she didn't know what was going on?

"You're quiet today," Mom said.

Becca smiled. "I was just thinking that we need to do

this more often. And next time Hayley really does have to be here."

"I absolutely agree." Mom reached over to squeeze her hand. "And Nika, too."

"She has important work, Mom," Buddy said, as he finally turned his attention to his own meal.

Becca bumped her shoulder against his. "Yeah. Maintaining the fleet of vehicles her billionaire boss owns is such important work."

Buddy had just picked up his fork and knife, but set them back down and turned to her. "Brendan Sloan is not her boss. And you have no idea how many lives her work impacts, so why don't you back off."

"Jeez, Buddy." Becca rolled her eyes. "I'm just saying, it seems like she should be able to get away every once in a while to spend time with your family. Especially since it's looking like we're going to be her family, too, someday."

Dad broke into the conversation. "All the more reason for you to give her a break, Becca."

"I think what Becca is trying to say is that we'd all like to get to know her better," Mom said. "But we can be patient. And we can be civil at our own family dinner, since those also don't happen as often as we'd like." She cast a pointed look at Buddy and Becca.

"Sure thing, Mom," Becca said. He mumbled an agreement as well.

Sophie arched an eyebrow at Buddy and said, "Are you ever going to tell us how you landed such a classy woman as Nika?"

Buddy half-smiled as he lifted a bite of roast potato. "Through my cooking, of course."

Everyone laughed and some of the tension seemed to ease. Honestly, Becca hadn't meant to set Buddy off. She was just trying to tease him. Maybe goad him into opening up a bit.

He'd been so wound up lately. And he wasn't confiding in her like he used to. He was keeping secrets, and she hated that she couldn't pry them out of him.

The conversation had just started again, although a little more subdued, when Buddy's watch started beeping. He set down his utensils and looked up at the ceiling.

"You gotta be kidding me," he mumbled. He somehow managed to swallow the bite he'd just taken and stood, backing away from the table. "I have to take this."

Becca swiveled around in her chair to watch him retreat. "Seriously? During family dinner?"

"I'll be quick," he yelled, already in the kitchen.

Mom reached over to squeeze Becca's hand again. "Come on, honey. Leave him be."

"Yeah, Becca," Sophie said. "Buddy's never had a girlfriend before. Give him time to work things out."

"If he keeps on like this, by the time he works things out, we'll never see him," Amy, their youngest sibling, stated sharply. "I get that Nika is important to him, but he needs to remember that we're important, too."

"Let's hear it for baby sis." Becca raised her glass just as another wave of goosebumps rocketed across her body. This time, they *started* on her spine and radiated out to cover her back.

What the hell was going on? To make things even more confusing, tingling warmth spread through her stomach and pooled in her belly and…lower.

That was awkward.

The Pomeranians both leapt from their beds and ran to the foyer, yapping loudly. Even Dash sat up, her ears perked in their direction. Mom yelped as someone pounded on the door. Not knocked, *pounded*. Becca swore she felt the floor shake beneath her feet with each blow.

"What the…" Mom pressed a hand to her chest. "What is it now?"

"I'll get it." Sophie rose, gave Dash the signal to stay put, then headed toward the living room.

It must be nice having a dog that listened.

"So much for a peaceful family dinner," Dad said.

Buddy hurried back from the kitchen. He didn't sit down. Instead, he grabbed Becca's arm and started pulling her out of her seat.

"We have to go," he said. "Now."

The urgency in his voice gave Becca a chill. She'd never seen such a serious expression on her big brother's face. Not even when he'd caught her making out with Brock Masters under the bleachers and dragged her back to their high school.

"What the hell is wrong with you?" Becca said. "I'm not leaving."

Why had he singled *her* out?

"Becca, I don't—" His face paled as he looked across the table. "Where's Sophie?"

"She went to answer the door." Amy pointed toward the open archway between the living room and dining room with a fork laden with roast. They had a clear view to the entry area.

"Buddy, what has gotten into you?" Mom said.

From the other room, Becca heard Sophie gasp, then say, "Oh my God."

Another wave of molten heat flooded through Becca. She pushed Buddy away, standing on her own and turning to face the front door. She could see Sophie, but not whoever was standing outside.

Dazzle ran back into the dining room and dove into her bed with a whimper. Pickles, though, was spinning in circles, a huge smile on his doggie face. He usually only reacted that way to family.

The Pomeranian darted out the door and a booming male voice said, "Pickles! I've missed you, my fierce friend."

Whoever it was, he had a great voice. Deep and rumbly

in a way that set her off even more than she already was.

The goosebumps escalated, tingles spreading through her in waves. Her mouth grew dry and she had to work to swallow.

Sophie was making half-formed sounds as she tried to speak. This guy must be something else, if he could render the chattiest of the siblings speechless.

"I am Kral," he said. "I'm here for Becca."

What the...?

"I'm... I'm Becca," Sophie stammered.

"No, she's not," Becca yelled. Of all the times to try that trick.

Even though they were born a year apart, Sophie and Becca were mistaken for twins all the time. Sophie sometimes used their similar appearances to fool people into thinking she was the older sister.

Becca had grown so tired of explaining that they just had some strong genetics going on in their family that she didn't even always correct people. She was definitely going to in this case.

Amy also looked a lot like them, with the same dark hair and brown eyes that all the girls had. Thankfully, as the surprise addition to the family, she was ten years younger than Sophie, so no one mistook them for triplets.

"Right, I'm Sophie." Sophie leaned closer to the dining room so the door was blocking her face from the stranger's view. She turned to look at Becca, mouthing, "Oh my

God," in a comically exaggerated way.

"Sophie, yes," the man—Kral—said. "One of Buddy's other sisters."

What the hell kind of name was Kral, anyway?

Becca's heartbeat kicked up. She had trouble remembering to breathe. Her skin prickled into more goosebumps.

Hearing his voice made a very pleasant heat build deep in her belly and brought a strange ache to her chest. An ache she mercilessly stomped.

Men were trouble. Especially hot men. Becca got her fill of them on nights when she hung out with Amy at The Parched Flamingo where Amy tended bar. They had both listened to way too many victory stories from drunk guys talking about conquests and seen too many women taken in by a gorgeous face or a smoking body. Judging by Sophie's reaction, this guy must be sizzling.

"May I enter?" Kral asked.

"Sure," Sophie said.

At the same time, Buddy yelled, "No, you may not."

Buddy let go of Becca's arm and started toward the door, but Sophie was already opening it wider. Becca wanted to grab Buddy to stop him and tell him he was being rude, but she was frozen in place.

The man outside—because he was still outside— stepped into the house. He hadn't been blocked by the door at all. In fact Becca wasn't sure it could hide him if he tore it of the hinges and held the thing in front of him, which he looked absolutely capable of doing.

He ducked under the lentil, gripping it with one huge hand as he did, as if to help gauge how low it was compared to his head. Pickles was tucked against his chest, resting in the crook of Kral's arm and smiling like the happiest pup in the world.

Becca could hardly blame him.

Once Kral was inside, he stood. His entire head was above the height of the door. If he rose up on his toes, she was pretty sure he'd bonk the ceiling.

Sophie backed away a step, her eyes wide as she stared at him. He turned to shut the door, giving Becca a great view of his broad back, tight backside, and sculpted legs. The jeans he wore were so tight, she could see the lines of muscle pressing against the fabric.

Where the hell did he find clothes in his size?

He wore metal wristbands that would have looked dorky on anyone else, but he somehow managed to pull off. They weren't quite chrome, but reflected the light almost as well.

His hair was more a mane of dark brown, broken into wavy strands with highlights like someone who spent most of their time in the ocean and sun. He turned around, revealing a beard that completed the wild and windblown look, and a necklace of shining, clear crystals that rested on his chest, complete with some kind of amulet in the center.

What a weirdo. A super-atomic-hot weirdo.

With his shoulders hunched a bit, towering over Sophie, Becca should have found him menacing as fuck. If a guy who looked like this walked into the sub shop when she was managing it, she would immediately be on high alert. But instead, more of that molten fire poured through her veins.

He looked over at her, his eyes a deep shade of orange that she'd never seen on anyone before. She swore he made a low, deep growl that she felt more than heard.

Then he was walking toward her and the rest of the world seemed to vanish. It was just her and this giant, hulking, gorgeous guy, falling toward each other like—

"Hey, Kral, this isn't a good time." Buddy stepped between them, breaking the spell.

Becca could finally move again. She used her newly recovered mobility to step to Buddy's side, which, unfortunately put her much closer to Kral. All the hair on her arms stood on end, like he was putting out some kind of electrical field that was giving her all kinds of tingles.

"Don't be ridiculous," Kral said. "Time can neither be good nor bad. It simply is." He kept staring into Becca's eyes, even though he was speaking to Buddy.

"Oh, my," Mom said, her voice breathier than usual.

A broad smile broke out on Kral's face, his teeth gleaming brightly against his light brown skin. He finally broke eye contact, turning to walk over to their mom. He held up a small bouquet of wilted wildflowers.

"These are for you," he said.

Mom tittered. Becca had never heard anyone titter before, but she was sure that's what it sounded like. She could understand where it was coming from.

"Amy, run and get another place setting," Mom said.

"Don't bother." Buddy shook his head vigorously, but Amy was already on her way to the kitchen. "Kral was just leaving."

"But he just got here," Sophie whined.

"Nonsense." Dad stood up and patted Amy on the shoulder as she passed him. "We have a feast here. It'd be wrong not to share it."

"He can sit next to me," Sophie said.

Wow, Sophie was really calling dibs on the new guy. Which was nothing new.

What *was* new was the way the thought of Sophie claiming this guy set Becca's teeth on edge.

Amy returned from the kitchen with a plate, glass, and utensils. She was even balancing an extra glass on the plate for the flowers. Mom rose from her seat to help get the extra place setting laid while Dad brought in an extra chair.

"It does smell spectacular," Kral said. "But then, your cooking has brought you fame throughout the galaxy." He laughed and slapped Buddy on the back, sending her "big" brother stumbling forward a few paces.

Buddy was usually the biggest guy in the room. Is was so weird to see him dwarfed by this guy.

Even weirder, her brother seemed almost desperate for Kral to leave. Becca had no idea why. Another secret. But this one, she had a chance to dig into.

"Come on, Buddy," she said, smirking. "We can't turn your friend away from your famous cooking."

She rested her hand on Kral's elbow, intending to steer him around the table to the spot between Amy and Sophie that they were already setting up. The moment her fingers touched his skin, the tingles she'd been feeling before amped up to full-on lightning strikes coursing along her nerve endings. She was almost dizzy from it.

Kral sucked in a quick breath, staring down at her again, his orange eyes seeming to glow. His lips twitched away from his teeth as his features took on a feral cast that made her toes curl.

He stepped closer, lifting a hand as if he meant to touch her face. She found herself wondering what it would be like to feel his huge hands tangled in her hair and—

"Okay, everything is ready." Sophie's sharp voice cut into the moment.

Becca stepped away from Kral, trying to steady her breathing. He kept that intense eye contact for a few moments, then turned and headed toward the opposite side of the table, where they'd set his place.

Sophie glared at Becca as they sat again. Becca couldn't bring herself to care. Her nerves were still lit up like a fireworks show.

Yeah, this guy was trouble with a capital 'T.'

—

I adore these warriors and can't wait to share more of their stories with you. *Kral: A Scifi Alien Warriors Romance* is just over the horizon!

If you want to learn more about Nuar and the other Cygnian warriors' universe, you can check out *The Department of Homeworld Security* adventures. Many of the novellas have been collected in the first two series omnibuses, *The Department of Homeworld Security Omnibus 1* and *The Department of Homeworld Security Omnibus 2*. Or you can pick and choose with the individual novellas.

I'd love to keep in touch. Join my newsletter at sendfox.com/cassandrachandler to hear about all the adventures happening in Cassland. And if you enjoyed this book, please consider leaving a review at your favorite book review site. I'd really appreciate it—reviews help readers and authors alike!

Thank you for reading *Nuar: A Scifi Alien Warriors Romance!*

Cassandra Chandler

About the Author

USA Today Bestselling author Cassandra Chandler uses her vivid imagination to make the world more interesting, spawning the ideas she turns into her whimsical Science Fiction Romances and darkly evocative Paranormal and Urban Fantasy Romances. Fast-paced and funny, lighthearted or dark, her stories will introduce you to characters you'll fall in love with and worlds you long to explore.